The Last Ram

To Mary Ann

I hope you enjoy

The Last Ram

A Novel of the Badlands

Steve Linstrom

NORTH STAR PRESS OF ST. CLOUD, INC.

St. Cloud, Minnesota

To Molly and Steph

Copyright © 2013 Steve Linstrom

ISBN: 978-0-87839-693-1

First Edition: June 2013

Printed in the United States of America

Published by
North Star Press of St. Cloud, Inc.
P.O. Box 451
St. Cloud, MN 56302

www.northstarpress.com   Facebook - North Star Press   Twitter - North Star Press

Acknowledgments

The road to a first novel is always difficult and I've been very fortunate to have a great deal of help along the way. The *Writer's Digest* classes taught me the basics of writing craft, thanks to the critiques of fellow classmates L. Mad Hildebrand, Lori Kaufman and Bob Mathias. My Northern Colorado Writers online critique group of Kathleen Murphy, Jennifer Carter, Lynn Carlson, Julia Lynne and Beth Eikenbary went through the book chapter by tortuous chapter. Placing in the Amazon Breakthrough Writers contest as a quarterfinalist in 2009 and 2010 gave me confidence and connected me with a great support group of Scott Armstrong, Ian Wilson, Kari Miller, Lizzie Ross, Jenny Milchman and of course, our fearless leader, Francsca Miller. They will all be on the bestseller list soon. Dana Yost was one of the first to read the whole novel and provided wonderful editorial feedback. Brad Nixon and Mary Vincent walked through the entire novel with an editor's eye and Casey Johnson did the initial cover design. Of course, the great folks at North Star Press brought all the pieces together and created the final product. Most of all, I'm very thankful for family for accompanying me on this long journey.

Prologue

THE OLD RAM COULD SENSE when a man was in the Badlands. After all these years he immediately knew how close, how dangerous and how best to avoid. Before a man had any idea of his presence, he could take two strides up a sheer cliff and be over the crest, barely leaving a mark in the hard, dry clay of the Badlands.

But today, for some reason, the ram lingered on the barren saddle framed by the craggy spires. He stood very still and waited.

The boy clawed at the loose clay in the dry creek bed below. He was struggling to scale a bank that could be cleared by the ram in a single bound. Gasping for breath, he finally pulled himself to a sprawl across the low embankment and raised his head.

At the top of the ravine, less than fifty yards away, the ram stood proudly, silhouetted against the evening sky. He had seen many men in the Badlands, but few had seen him. Until today.

It had been many seasons since there were other sheep to warn of intruders. The brother rams he had fought in these valleys were gone. The springtime clash of the great horns echoing off the spires would never be heard again. The ewes he had battled for and won and the lambs that came from them could no longer be protected. Their time was over. They were all gone. Now the deer and coyotes and hawks and rattlesnakes and the little animals roamed, but no sheep. And the men. Season after season, spring after spring, the men kept coming.

The ram slowly turned. The last rays of the sun kissed the great horns wrapped around the sides of his head. His large golden eyes scanned down the ravine and contemplated the single boy on the ridge, surrounded by the harsh spires and ridges and washes of the Badlands. He stood motionless as an ancient idol, his breath forming a mist above him and rising into the twilight sky.

He lifted his nose and drew in the cool evening air. Then with a single powerful bound, he was over the ridge and gone.

Chapter One

THE DOOR EXPLODED OPEN and Evan entered the dusty store in a flurry of skinny arms, legs and oversized feet.

"Pa, you should have seen the sheep I saw! It was huge." He shrugged out of his coat in full stride and threw it at the hook on the wall, missing by a mile. He left the tattered and patched coat slumped in a dark corner. The floor of the old store creaked as he rushed toward the two men playing checkers by the light of a flickering kerosene lamp.

James Warner's eyes remained half-closed as he glanced up from the dimly lit checker board. "Mrs. Blake was in here looking for you again," he said in a low, slow voice. "Your mother won't be happy to hear you were out wandering the Badlands like an Indian when you were supposed to be in school."

Warner pushed the long, thin strands of his hair away from his forehead and turned back to the board. His slight fingers, placed carefully at his temples, created shadows in the lines framing his face. At forty-five, he had lost his youthfulness, but had not acquired the look of wisdom that comes with experience.

"I was scouting deer for when David comes home," Evan said, bouncing on his toes as he leaned against the wall by the table. He deftly ignored his father's comments about school. He'd worry about Mrs. Blake and the one room school later. "But you should've seen it, Pa. It was a huge ram. It had horns that went around like this." His hands whirled in circles along the side of his head, knocking into an empty shelf. "Up below Mystic Table, by the Stronghold it—"

"Damn it, Evan, you're going to knock that shelf down!" his father snapped, looking directly at him for the first time. "It's 1903, and there aren't any bighorn sheep left in the Badlands. They were hunted out twenty years ago. It must've been a whitetail buck." He returned to the checkerboard, massaging his temples and muttering half under his breath, "You're thirteen, for God's sake. Act it."

"I know what a buck looks like," Evan said through tight lips, leaning over the checker board and partially blocking the light from the little lamp. A drop of sweat rolled off his chin and hit the board as he continued. "I'm telling you, it was a sheep!"

Evan stood with his hands clenched into fists at his side. His father waved a hand at the shadow across the board, signaling for him to move, but Evan didn't care.

The other player at the table, Morgan, took a small sip of cheap whiskey—his usual drink—and pushed his battered cowboy hat up high on his forehead. The old chair creaked as he tipped it back against the wall, lifting the front legs off the floor. Morgan's small blue eyes studied the boy intently from beneath his thick gray-blonde eyebrows. "There used to be good sized sheep in the Badlands," he said in his slow drawl. "Indians put great store by them. Said they had the power to show the future. Haven't seen any sign of 'em in years." Morgan rarely spoke more than a few words. James looked up from the game and watched the old rancher's craggy face with interest.

Evan faced the old rancher. "I saw him, Mr. Morgan. I know I saw him. He had horns that wrapped all around his head and he was as big as a buck. I'm telling you, he had these huge horns and he stopped at the top of the ridge and he looked back and went over the top and . . ." His voice slowly trailed off under Morgan's gaze.

Evan knew it had to be a sheep. He'd seen a picture of a bighorn sheep in one of the books in Mrs. Blake's school room. The animal book was the only book in the "school library" that interested him.

"Could be," Morgan drawled, nodding his head and sucking at his teeth. "The Badlands is a rough place. There's valleys and draws out there that no man has ever seen or remembered. And I've seen huge dark cracks and ravines that could swallow a man up. Next rainstorm, the whole crack is caved in and there'll be a whole new valley formed. Could be an ol' ram stayed out there all these years." He continued to study the boy as he slowly rocked back and forth on the back legs of the chair.

Abruptly, he let out a cough and swung forward, thudding the front chair legs on the ground. He pulled out his gold watch and studied it. "I'll go out and look tomorrow," he said without looking up.

"You'll see, Mr. Morgan." Evan pressed again, extending his shadow over the board. "You'll see him! He was by the Stronghold by Mystic Ridge. He—"

Morgan looked up, his eyes flashing. "I said I'd get out there." He turned back to the game.

"Evan, quit bothering me and Morgan," his father said in a flat voice. "You'd better get back to the house and explain to your mother where you've been."

"Yessir." Evan lowered his eyes. He walked to the very back of the store, dragging his feet, forgetting the dirty coat on the floor by the front door. Looking back, he saw that Morgan had pulled his hat back down low over his eyes. His father had placed his head back in his hands. The back door creaked as Evan pulled it open, and he intentionally let it slam as he entered the cluttered lean-to connecting the store to the small house.

The smell of stew filled his nose as he carefully picked his way through the dark lean-to. He pushed open the door to the house and gave his mother a confident smile. "Hi, Mom. Dinner smells great," he said as he slid into the nearest chair.

His mother, Deloris, looked up from the pot she was stirring. Her dark hair, tied back with a blue scarf, was just starting to show gray streaks. Her faded print dress looked exactly like the one she wore every weekday. Evan never really considered if it was the same one.

"Don't 'Hi Mom' me, Evan Theodore Warner," she snapped, her blue eyes flashing. "Mrs. Blake said you skipped out of lessons again this afternoon. She was over here right after school to find you, and I was embarrassed to death."

Evan lowered his eyes and slumped further into the chair by the kitchen table. He slid it back as far as he could against the wall. The kitchen always felt small, but at times like this it seemed even smaller.

"But Mom, David's coming back this week, and I need to scout where we'll hunt." Evan spread his hands across the table. "He'll only be here for a few weeks. We have to get a big buck before he goes back to that school. And Mom, you should have seen the ram I saw. He—" He waved his hands in circular motions as he started to describe the ram's enormous horns.

"I don't care about your hunting," she interrupted, wiping a stray strand of hair back from her face. "David's coming home to visit Mr. and Mrs. Blake, not to go cavorting around the Badlands with you. He's probably outgrown all of that wild Indian foolishness and applied himself to his studies. Unlike you, I may add." She raised an eyebrow and gave him a hard look. "You know, you have got to apply yourself or you'll end up a wandering soul living from day to day, year to year, and not getting anywhere." She turned back to the hot smoking stove.

Silence hung in the room. She had not said "like your father," but Evan had a sense she'd wanted to.

"So," she finally asked, breaking the tension, "What were you doing out there in that godforsaken place?" She dished out a bowl of stew for Evan and wiped her hands on her apron. The wonderful smell of the stew filled the kitchen.

"Like I told you, I was scouting," he said blowing steam off the hot meat and potatoes, thankful she had moved the conversation away from school. "David's coming back next week and we want to get back to the Badlands like old times." He spooned the stew to his mouth with great relish. It was hot and he was hungry, but he was also anxious to keep his mother's attention thoughts away from school. She was always in a better mood when he tied right into her cooking.

She sat across the table tending to the endless task of keeping the family in decent clothes. "I swear, you grow out of these pants faster than I can lengthen them. It would be easier to just shorten your legs." A small smile passed across her face. Then her voice hardened again. "I doubt that Mrs. Blake is going to let David run off into the Badlands with you and act like a wild Indian after she sent him off to school to get educated and all respectable."

"I wish he hadn't gone off to that fancy Indian school." Evan made a slurping sound as he sucked the hot stew off his spoon. "Why couldn't he have just stayed here and gone to school with me?"

"You know that when the Blakes got him from the Indians, they agreed to get the best education for him," his mother said. "At that school he can interact with other progressive Indian boys and have a chance to make something of himself." She sounded like she was reciting a speech.

Evan didn't know what "progressive" was, but he thought it must have to do with not hunting and exploring like the other Indian kids on the reservation. He decided that he must not be very progressive either because he would much rather be in the Badlands than sitting in a boring classroom.

"Mom, where's David's real parents? I mean his Indian ones," he asked between bites. "And why did they leave him with the Blakes?" Evan had a habit of thinking of something one minute and saying it the next without really thinking it through.

His mother looked up at him and her temper flared again.

"Indians, Indians, Indians, I've told you a hundred times to stop talking about Indians! You act like you're one of those damned Indians yourself with no respect for learning, no respect for money, no ambition." The light from the lamp flickered off her face, hard as ivory. "That's why the Blakes sent David away to school, to get the Indian out of him. And here you are acting worse than any of them, skipping school to traipse around the Badlands! Why, I've never been so embarrassed in my life."

"Mom," he said, keeping his eyes low. He was used to this lecture by now and knew her irritation would pass. "I just wanted to . . ."

She'd turned her eyes back to her sewing, and Evan could see her face flushing pink. She looked across the table at him, and said quietly, "I think his mother's dead and his father was having a hard time. Something about the Sioux Wars." She leaned forward. "Those days are over and some of them just can't change. They aren't like us."

Evan watched his mother as she quickly straightened her back and returned to her sewing. He hadn't expected an answer from her, but had noticed that she was talking to him more like a real adult lately. "Maybe I'll ask David sometime, or maybe Morgan."

He couldn't help but smile remembering those hot summer days exploring the Badlands before David got sent away to be "progressive."

They'd come back to town covered with dirt, dust and mud, but full of stories of adventure, some real and most made up. "Sometimes I think you are more wild Indian than that Indian kid," his mother would say when they got back.

"It's been two whole years since I've seen David. I wonder if he's changed."

The boys had exchanged a few letters, but writing was difficult and time consuming for Evan. He tried to tell David everything he'd seen and done and how adventures weren't the same without him, but the few sentences he managed to scribble never seemed very real. David's return letters from the Pierceson School for Indian Boys had become fancier and fancier and he wrote about things Evan didn't understand. The words, in perfect penmanship on the crisp, white paper, looked like they came out of one of his lesson books. He couldn't imagine David talking that way. His natural charm and athletic ability had evidently served him well because he wrote about being on the boxing team and becoming a house supervisor, whatever that was.

"David hasn't seen the Badlands in forever, Mom. I know he'll want to spend every second out there with me, especially when he hears about the ram."

His mother didn't look up from her sewing. Her blush faded and she'd gone back to the hard look. "I don't care what you saw. Neither of you should be wasting your time running around the Badlands like wild Indians. You aren't an Indian and David went to school to get over all that. You need to spend your time learning some respectability. It's the 1900s, for goodness' sake. You can't act like a heathen savage." The needle clicked against the thimble on her finger. "If you skip out of Mrs. Blake's class again, your father will whip the wildness right out of you."

It was a pretty empty threat. His father hadn't whipped him—ever. Administering a whipping would require significant planning, forethought, and exertion, none of which were his father's strengths.

"Yes, Mom," he sighed as he crossed the small room to the kitchen bucket. He washed up his dishes, cleaned his face and headed to bed.

THE NEXT DAY, Evan had a more difficult time than usual with his lessons at school. As much as he tried, he couldn't keep the ram a secret and told everyone in the class what he'd seen. Mrs. Blake told him he could look up the picture in the animal book in the library if he got all his arithmetic problems right. He tried harder than ever, but he just couldn't do it. As usual, Emily Johnson did and gave him one of her superior know-it-all smiles. When Mrs. Blake wouldn't let him look at the book, he vowed to steal it next chance he got.

When she finally let the class go, they stampeded out of the little building behind of the Blakes's house that served as the school. Evan was the first to cross the rutted main street to the store.

Morgan was already there tying his horse, Blue, to the railing running across the front of the boardwalk. Word had spread of his mission, and several people were standing in front of the store, waiting for the old rancher to speak. James Warner leaned against the doorway of the store watching the activity, wiping his hands on a rag.

It was unusual for Morgan to talk in front of so many people. He rested his elbow on Blue's saddle. "Ain't no doubt about it. Those were sheep tracks up on Mystic Table. Big 'un too," he said, removing his leather gloves and shoving them into a saddlebag. "I ain't seen tracks like that for years." His thick eyebrows danced under his hat and his eyes shone bright blue.

Evan beamed.

"Them tracks were right there in a mud wallow at the top of the ravine," Morgan said, pointing to a spot on the ground in front of him. Everyone in the crowd leaned over to look in the dirt. "Right where Evan said they'd be. You wouldn't ever notice them less you were lookin' for them real specific like."

"Why haven't we seen any of these big sheep before?" Emily Johnson asked, edging herself in front of the other kids and dramatically sweeping her blond hair over her shoulder. She always had to ask the first question. Even though she was a year younger than Evan, she acted and talked like she was much older.

"The cattle drove them out of the prairie and into the Badlands where they either starved or got hunted out, I reckon." Morgan pounded at his pants, creating little dust storms. Mrs. Bittiman frowned and stepped back to avoid the dust but stayed close enough to hear.

"Did the Injuns kill them all?" asked Jimmie Baxter, his brown eyes open wide. Eight years old and full of energy, he was always running everywhere and sticking his nose into everyone's business.

"Naw, the Indians put great store by them sheep. One story says that the sheep all went into one of those deep cracks in the Badlands to provide food for the souls of the lost Sioux Nation." Morgan raised his eyebrows, looked at the children and dropped his voice very low. "An' when the time is right, an' the moon is full, the ghosts of all them dead Indians will come streaming outta the Badlands and scalp all the young'uns in the country." He raised his hands over his head and wriggled his fingers. "Whooo whoooo."

He lowered his arms and hugged his stomach. His whole body shook, and he made a dry, cackling noise. Evan thought that it was first time he'd ever heard Morgan laugh.

The group silently watched the old rancher shake until Mrs. Baxter broke the silence. "Really, Mr. Morgan, how could you scare the children so?" she scolded, putting her arm around young Jimmie. "Now you just tell these children that you were joking so they don't have nightmares. Scalping Indians indeed!"

Morgan stopped cackling, and his face fell. He reached into his pocket, pulled out his watch and studied it intently. "Stories been around for years," he mumbled, still staring at his watch. "Same stories, year after year. Ain't none of them true. Damn fool kids should know that." He closed his watch case with a snap, making everyone jump, and stepped up onto the wooden walkway. He brushed past James without another word and disappeared into the store.

"Evan, tell us again about how you seen it!" Jimmie Baxter pulled on the front of Evan's shirt.

He launched into the story, leading the other children and a few of the adults into the store. Even Emily Johnson was listening to him.

After a while, the attention started to tire him. The more times he told the story, the bigger the ram got and the redder his face got. He felt his ears burn hot as he mimicked the swirl of the horns for the fifth time in an hour to Jimmie and the younger kids. If they paid any attention, they would've heard it the first time. As he started telling the story again, out of the corner of his eye he noticed Emily slipping out the door.

"A trophy like that would bring a pretty penny, I bet." A trapper from north of the Cheyenne River named Jeffers was leaning against the front counter. "Why don't you show me where you saw the critter, and I'll give you ten percent of whatever I sell the head fer?"

Evan pictured the bloody head of the great ram staining the back counter. "I don't remember exactly," he lied and lowered his eyes. "All the draws look the same out there. I think it was on the south . . . no, the east end."

"Ah hell, you don't know nothin'," Jeffers said with a wave of his hand, ruining Evan's momentary hero status. He shook his head, swore underneath his breath, and stomped out.

The crowd in the store went silent after Jeffers left. The other kids began to file out of the store without looking at Evan, and he felt his face burn again.

He slowly made his way over to the table in the back of the store where Morgan was sitting beneath the small window. Head down, Morgan sipped from the little glass of whiskey in front of him and moved a black checker from one space to the next and back. Evan could sense the cowboy was miffed about being rebuked by the Baxter woman. Besides that, all of the commotion had disrupted the start of his checkers game, as James had the unusual job of tending to customers.

"Mr. Morgan, do you think someone will shoot the ram?" Evan asked, leaning against the wall. He'd not been asked to sit.

Morgan continued to move the black checker, pushing it around the borders of a single red space. "I reckon so," he said. You don't see a big animal like that very often in these parts." He took his finger off the checker and pulled out his watch.

"But why do we have to kill it? It isn't like we'd eat it for food."

Morgan leaned back in his chair, took a small sip of his drink, and looked up at Evan. "These parts have changed a whole lot since I first came out here. Used to be that we was just barely getting by with Indians, rain, snow and drought. Mother Nature's a rough old bitch. But we beat her. We got a roof for the weather, drinks in bottles and tame Indians. We got this place civilized so folks can live here," he said, waving his hand at the customers in the front of the store. "Not that they appreciate it. That sheep's just another piece of the chain left over from the old times. Somebody'll kill it. Ain't nothin' that can live forever."

"Who do you think will shoot it?" Evan asked in a quiet voice. He didn't like the image of the great head of the ram lying in a puddle of blood.

"I reckon folks from all over will come lookin' for it," Morgan drawled. "The last of anything's of considerable interest. They'll kill it all right, an' then they'll stuff it and parade it all over the country. They gotta show they won." He turned back to the board and resumed moving the black checker around. "Like winnin' matters," he mumbled to himself, shaking his head.

"How'll anybody find him if they don't know the Badlands?" Evan shifted his weight from foot to foot. He wished Morgan would ask him to sit down.

After a while, the old rancher's glanced up from under his hat like he'd just realized Evan was there. "I reckon they'll find someone from around here to guide them. Maybe one of the Indians."

"David and I know the Badlands better than anyone but you," Evan said with a frown. "Better than any Indian. Besides, they won't guide no white man to the ram."

Morgan fixed his gaze on Evan. "There's Indians and there's Indians," he said. "Puttin' them all together don't make sense. Are you the same as that pesky Baxter kid?" he asked, pointing to the front of the store. "Besides, did you forget that David's an Indian?"

Evan shot back, "David ain't a real Indian, he's my friend. He ain't like the reservation kids."

Morgan looked back down at the table and started moving the chip around again. Evan waited silently for him to answer. For what seemed an eternity, the only sound was the checker sliding across the board.

"Mr. Morgan, how did David come to live with the Blakes instead'a with the Indians?" Evan asked softly. "David never told me. I know his father was in the Indian Wars."

Morgan's breathing was slow and rhythmic. He lifted his head and looked toward the late afternoon light streaming through the dirty window. Evan was surprised when he started talking.

"His daddy's name was Stone Eagle," he said finally. "And shootin' don't make a war."

"I've never heard of an Indian named Stone Eagle."

Indians wandered through town all the time. The reservation was only a few miles away. They kept pretty much to themselves and left the whites alone, but everybody knew each other. There was always the rumor of a "ghost tribe" that lived in the Badlands and never went to the reservation, but Evan doubted it. There was nothing to eat in the Badlands.

"Stone Eagle was differ'nt than the tame Indians we've got around here these days," Morgan said. "He didn't give a damn about nothin' or nobody."

Evan thought the lines running down the sides of the old rancher's face looked like the little ravines that formed after a gully washer hit in the Badlands. "How come I never seen him around?" he finally asked, squirming his back against the wall.

Morgan rocked back in his chair, his face now fully lit by the single shaft of late afternoon light in the shadowy store. "Stone Eagle was at Wounded Knee. When the Army killed all those Indians, they didn't kill him. He never got over it."

"You mean he was there and saw it all?" Evan asked, sliding into the other chair without being asked.

"He lived it. His family was part of Big Foot's band."

Morgan's voice dropped lower than usual, his eyes closed against the light of the window. "After Wounded Knee, Stone Eagle and David was about the only ones of his family left."

Evan stared at the old rancher's face, worn and craggy in the late afternoon light. "He's still alive? Why doesn't he live out on the reservation with the other Indians?"

"He ain't never been able to settle down. One day he dropped his kid off with the Blakes and we ain't seen him since."

Evan shifted his feet impatiently. "Mr. Blake told everyone that David's father was dead."

"Guess he mostly was, or is. A thing like that kills something inside a man," Morgan mumbled as he got his watch out and held it open over his stomach.

"Does David know? Why didn't he ever tell me?" Evan whispered, partly to himself, leaning eagerly over the table.

"It's the Blakes's business and David's." Morgan looked up from his watch. "I reckon I've said too much already. If he wanted you to know, he'd a told you." The light from the window faded with a passing cloud.

"How do you know so much about Stone Eagle?" Evan asked as Morgan turned his attention back to the checker board.

"Wounded Knee," Morgan said, his voice rumbling from deep in his throat. "I was there too." He looked up, one blue eye staring intently from under the tilted brim of his hat. Then he looked down at his watch once more, snapped it shut and put it back in his pocket.

He rose and quietly walked out of the store, leaving Evan alone in the dying light.

Chapter Two

A SUDDEN LURCH KNOCKED DAVID'S head against the train window, startling him awake. The train resumed its rhythmic, slow-moving dance through the endless South Dakota prairie. David's back ached from the hard wooden bench. As the fog of sleep cleared, he remembered that he'd been dreaming. He frowned, trying to bring the dream into focus.

He'd been conversing with someone, someone very old. And they'd been talking in Lakota.

David didn't know Lakota. Besides, at the Pierceson School, a boy could be whipped for uttering even a phrase in native Indian tongue. He'd long ago forgotten even the most rudimentary Lakota phrases. But in his dream, he understood the old voice perfectly. And when he responded, the words coming out of his mouth were in fluent Lakota. The memory faded so fast that he couldn't remember what the voice in the dream had told him or what he'd said in response. He just remembered listening and talking and that the voice was old.

He hoped he hadn't talked in his sleep.

The view out the window hadn't changed in hours. David still saw flat, gray-brown prairie interspersed with ambitious green fields of corn and beans. He pushed his jet black hair into place and wiped the hair oil from his hand on bottom of the wooden seat. Everything was flatter and more monotonous than he remembered . . . from when he was an Indian.

He checked on the man sitting across from him. Edmund Blake had no problem sleeping on a train or anywhere else. As usual, his bushy gray hair was in disarray as he slumped against the window snoring softly through his thick gray brush of a mustache. A drop of drool extended from the corner of his mouth, ready to drop to his shirt and join the stains from the tomato soup they'd had for lunch. David smiled as he thought about how mad Mrs. Blake would be. No matter what she did to dress him up, poor Mr. Blake always found a way to demonstrate his Ohio pig farmer roots.

Another lurch of the train sent a young man standing in the aisle careening into Mr. Blake. Without waking up, he rolled against the window and continued snoring.

The man mumbled an apology to the sleeping form and straightened up. He wore a light brown suit and a heavily starched white shirt. A notebook and several pencils stuck out of his jacket pocket. David thought he looked very prosperous.

"He seems to be able to sleep through anything," the man said with a smile, gesturing toward Mr. Blake. "Is he with you?"

David unconsciously straightened his tie. "Yes, Mr. Blake and I are returning to our home in Interior." David had quickly picked up the crisp diction taught by Professor Bonhomme at the Pierceson School for Indian Boys.

The young man raised his eyebrows and studied David. His starched white shirt and gray suit contrasted with his copper skin, dark eyes and shiny black hair. The black string tie was precisely knotted in the exact manner Professor Bonhomme had taught them all at school.

"So, you're from the reservation?" the man asked.

"I live with Mr. and Mrs. Blake." He pointed at the man across from him, running a self-conscious hand over his hair. It was cut "city" short, heavily greased and combed to the side in the prescribed manner. There seemed to be a prescribed manner for everything at the Pierceson School. There was a very specific path to success for an Indian in the white world, including proper haircut, clothing, manner of speaking, manner of walking and, as the students joked among themselves, manner of shitting.

Some of the students rebelled and complained about being forced to abandon their heritage and to never look or act like Indians. Every term two or three "Rez Indians" would demand their right to wear long hair and traditional clothing. They were soon removed from the school, never to be heard from again. David heard they were sent to one of the "farm schools," where they learned to be farmers by being hired out as laborers. It sounded more like a forced labor camp.

David sympathized with the "Rez" kids but no longer saw the point they were trying to make. Over the last two years he'd come to accept that acting white was just another way of acting.

"You don't look like most Indian kids," the young man said. "Are you going back to Interior to hunt the sheep?"

"I have been attending the Pierceson School for the last two years," David said. "And I don't know anything about a sheep."

The young man extended his hand and David shook it. "Mac Terrel, Sioux Falls *Argus Leader*." He shook hands with great vigor and David thought he really enjoyed saying his own name. "You haven't heard about the Audubon Sheep they found in the Badlands? Most of the people on the train today are trophy hunters." Terrel's eyes darted around to the other seats to see if anyone was listening. The two little old ladies in the back of the car continued to chat quietly and the other two men in the car slept.

David shook his head. "I ain't never seen any sheep in the Badlands," he said, falling into a rural dialect without thinking about it.

Terrel opened his notebook with great flourish. "It seems everyone thought the last Audubon Sheep was killed at least fifteen years ago. All the resources say it was an extinct species and the last anyone would see of it was in Mr. Audubon's famous painting. Then, there's a report that a ram was spotted in the Badlands last week. If there's one out there, it'll make quite a trophy." He snapped his notebook shut and looked up as if waiting for a comment.

"So you're looking for the sheep too?" David asked. He wasn't sure what Terrel wanted from him.

"Oh, of course not. I'm a journalist," Terrel pursed his thin lips and patted his notebook. "This is the biggest story the state of South Dakota has seen for years. My editor, Daniel Jameson, asked me personally to cover this event. I'm surprised you haven't seen any of my bylines from my introductory stories on the subject."

"What's so important about a sheep in the Badlands?" David asked, straightening his tie again. He knew more about the Badlands than any white person except old Morgan and maybe Evan Warner. He certainly knew more than this self-important twit from Sioux Falls, and he'd never seen any sheep out there.

"Why, it's the last of the species," Terrel said, a little too loudly. "For millions of years these noble creatures have roamed God's green Earth and now there is but a single one left. It is an honorable and epic story." He looked out of the corner of his eye to see if anyone but David was listening to him and frowned slightly when he saw they weren't.

To David, killing the last of the sheep didn't seem like an honorable thing to do, but he really couldn't say why. Both Indians and whites had killed game in the Badlands for as long as he could remember, until there wasn't much game left. Honor, one way or another, was never really a factor. There was food or there wasn't.

"Hunters from all over the world will converge on these desolate plains of Dakota to hunt the last of the wily sheep. Why, there's even a trophy hunter in the White House. T.R. himself may come out to hunt the sheep." Terrel was apparently trying out opening lines of his story. "The last of the species, using the guile and wit learned over the ages, competing for life against the best of modern technology. Inevitably, technology will win out and someone will be hailed as the greatest hunter of the new millennium. He'll tour the country with the trophy ram." Then almost to himself he said, "And someone will need to lead the tour to take the story to the country. Perhaps even write a book."

The door at the head of the train car banged open. A tall, thin man in a dark suit entered and held the door open, waiting. David caught a whiff of smoke curling into the car. All the passengers looked at the open door expectantly.

A short, thin man dressed in a rumpled, tan, linen suit nodded to the man holding the door and moved down the aisle. He walked with a deliberate grace, scanning the car with heavily hooded eyes. He ran a hand over his close-cropped blonde hair.

Terrel moved to the center of the aisle, blocking his way. "Colonel Lauper, sir, do you think you'll get the sheep?" he asked, fumbling for his notebook. "You've never hunted in this part of the country and it will certainly provide some unique challenges." Lauper looked at

Terrel's face, his suit and his shoes. "Wiiindsohrr, who is this puh-son?" he asked the man who had held the door and then followed him, demonstrating a pronounced upper class English accent. David thought he sounded bored or lazy.

"Mac Terrel, Sioux Fall *Argus Leader*," the reporter responded, holding up his notebook. "We're covering the—"

"What, pray tell, is an *Ahhhgus Leadeh*?" Lauper asked with raised eyebrows, turning to the reporter directly for the first time. He again ran a well-manicured hand over his short blonde hair.

Terrel gaped for a second and before he could answer, Lauper shrugged, slid past him and glided through door into the next car, with Windsor close behind him. As Terrel moved to follow them, a firm hand gripped his arm, stopping his progress. The hand belonged to a tall man with a weatherbeaten face.

"Ah'm Rafe Colton, Mr. Terrel," the man said in a loud voice. Ah reckon ah'll be guiding Colonel Lauper on this here hunt and can answer any questions you have." Colton wore a hat with a large brim pinned up on one side. With his thick red mustache and buckskin vest, he looked like he had stepped out of the cover of a dime novel.

"Colonel Lauper has hunted down trophy animals all over the world," Rafe continued. "When he heard about this last sheep, he came right down to my show and says to me, 'Rafe, you are the onliest man I know that can guide me right to that there sheep.' An' I told him he was right. Heh, Heh." He slapped Terrel on the back. "Ah tol' him that—"

"Excuse me, sir," the dark-suited man named Windsor said from the other end of the car, his mouth screwed up like he'd just bitten into a lemon. "Colonel Lauper would like you to follow us, Mr. Colton. We need to discuss provisioning."

"Ah yep, Windsor, Ah'll be right there," Colton said, still holding Terrel's shoulder. "I was just telling—"

"Colonel Lauper said specifically now, sir." Windsor turned on his heel and glided through the back door of the car with his chin raised high.

"Windsor is Lauper's servant man," Colton rasped under his breath. "He thinks he runs the show. I best go keep those Englishmen out of trouble." As he departed, he proclaimed loud enough for the entire car to hear, "Be seeing you, Mr. Terrel of the *Argus Leader*. That's Rafe R-A-F-E Colton, C-O-L-T-O-N, wilderness scout, Indian fighter and big game hunter extraordinaire." He clapped Terrel on the back one more time and sauntered down the aisle with the fringes on his coat swinging. He did a double take as he passed David but said nothing.

"Who was that?" David asked Terrel as the reporter came back up the aisle.

Terrel laughed. "Why that's Rafe Colton, wilderness scout, Indian fight—"

"No, not the great scout," David interrupted with a laugh. "The Englishman."

"Colonel Daniel Lauper is one of the foremost hunters in the world," Terrel said, screwing up his face as he made a show of recalling all the facts. "According to what I've read, he has a trophy warehouse back in England somewhere. One of my sources told me he might be coming out on this train. If he's hunting the Audubon Sheep, he'll be the one to shoot it. It'll be a great story. I need to make sure I can be the one to accompany him and tell the world."

"And who or what was that great scout?" David asked.

"My bet is that he runs some sort of Wild West show back East and got himself hired on to guide." Terrel shook his head. "I hope Lauper doesn't think that he can appropriately publicize this hunt without professionals."

The back door to the train reopened and Windsor floated back up the aisle, looking straight ahead. He stopped in the middle of the car where Terrel stood, looking at him expectantly. Windsor pivoted abruptly to address David.

"Colonel Lauper noticed you and deduced that you might be familiar with the local terrain. Bad Lands, I believe it is called," he said in a his soft, precise voice.

"I'm from the Badlands," David answered leaning forward with interest to hear what the man was saying.

"Are you a local Indian? Colonel Lauper has found that local aboriginals are by far the best guides." Windsor had a way of simultaneously raising his chin and lowering his eyes to peer over his nose when he spoke.

"I'm not much interested in hunting anymore and I'm afraid there are not many local aboriginals left," David said dryly in his best English diction. "They seem to have been killed or starved. However, if you are paying money, my friend Evan Warner probably knows the Bad-lands as well as anyone. And I think he's Irish aboriginal," he added, keeping his face expressionless.

"Evan Warner," Windsor mused as he pulled a pad out of his pocket and wrote down the name. He turned on his heel and glided back down the aisle without another word.

Terrel, irked at being ignored by Windsor, spun around and re-turned to his seat in the front of the car. David shook his head and sat back in his seat. His trip to Interior was not going to be as boring as he'd thought. He pictured the towering spires of the Badlands and for an instant felt the dry clay crackling at his feet. He looked down at his stiff, well-polished shoes. They weren't the shoes of an Indian.

Not surprisingly, Edmund Blake had slept through the entire episode.

Chapter Three

*I*T STARTS WITH DARK *and cold, biting cold. Always. The darkness fades into gray smoke, all-encompassing thick gray smoke that fills his lungs, stealing his breath and bringing tears to his eyes. The harsh sulfur smell of gunpowder sears his nose. The roar of gunfire engulfs him. Rolling thunder, individual shots rolled into a single wall of noise. Through the smoke, glimpses of children and women and soldiers against the snow. His heart pounds in terror and fear and shame. The cold has frozen his joints and robbed him of his voice. He can't run, he can't move, he can't yell, he can only watch. Then . . . he's left waiting for the smoke to clear, fearing what it might reveal.*

Stone Eagle sat up with a jerk and bashed his head into the rough face of the granite outcropping. It was a strong, protective comfort when he fell asleep, but now was a cold, hard wall against his face. His head throbbed and he felt the beginnings of a knot on his forehead.

He sat against the boulder with his arms around his knees. Years of experience had taught him that no matter what, he must stay awake until dawn. He cowered against the base of the rock with his hand inside his shirt, fingers grasping a leather pouch against his chest.

A half-moon illuminated the scene around him in a ghostly gray light. A few feet below him, the ledge on which he had slept ended and the plains stretched out miles to the east. He was over a thousand feet above the floor of the pale, grassy sea. Looking up, he made out the peak of Bear Butte, tall and ominous in the moonlight, a quarter-mile away and five hundred feet higher.

The spirit of this massive fist of rock was supposed to take the dreams away. It was the spiritual center of the Lakota and he had hid from it for years. Desperately looking for peace, he had come here three days ago and climbed to this lair to rid himself of the horrible haunting burden. Three days with no food and only a bladder of water, and the dreams still overwhelmed him every night. They made his heart race, his body sweat and his mind scream in terror. Every night the dreams returned.

The water was gone now. It was time to descend Bear Butte in the light of day. The spirits of his ancestors had failed him—again. He tightened his grip on the leather pouch and waited for the comfort of dawn.

———————————————

FAR ACROSS THE PLAINS to the east, the sky turned from black to dark blue and then to gray. His head began to clear with the first welcome rays of sun. It was time to leave, but he didn't know where he could go. Home had been the abandoned mining cabins in the Black Hills that allowed him to drop out of sight. Deadwood and the other mining communities in the northern hills provided opportunities for whiskey, and whiskey stopped the dreams. He held up his hand and looked at the bruises in the light of the sun's first rays. The blood splattered on his sleeve meant he couldn't go back, could no longer remain out of sight.

When there was enough light to make out the faint trail behind the outcropping, he staggered to his feet. His eyes swam in his head as he stumbled down the steep slope of the mountain. Three days of fasting had taken him past the point of gnawing hunger. He was just weak. His stamina gave out as the trail curved around the head of a ravine.

He stopped to rest and looked back at the ledge on which he had placed so much hope. Bear Butte hadn't stopped the dreams, he didn't have a vision and he was no better off than when he started. There might be Lakota spirits on Bear Butte, but they certainly had not come to rescue him. He supposed it was because he wasn't very Lakota anymore.

He turned and for the next hour, picked his way around the stones on the path to the bottom of the steep slope, keeping his back to the spirit's home, which had failed him. He staggered across the white man's road and lunged down the steep bank to the little stream that ran around the foot of Bear Butte. Falling face first into the creek, he drank until his stomach hurt. The cold, clear water revived him and eased the pounding in his head.

As he sat back against the bank of the little stream, a light scent of wood smoke drew his attention. He got up and followed the scent downstream, staying close to the thick wall of brush along the bank. The smell grew stronger as he came to a bend in the creek. Peering over a clump of chokecherry bushes, he saw a lone man, an Indian, sitting in front of a small fire. He was spooning cornmeal into his mouth from a tin plate.

Stone Eagle knew he should be cautious, especially after what happened in Deadwood, but hunger overrode his instinct. He stepped out from behind the bush and stood silently watching the man across the campsite.

He was younger than Stone Eagle, perhaps in his late twenties, and was dressed in the white man's clothing the Indian Agents distributed on the reservation. His hair was only six inches long and hung from his head like a mop.

Realizing that he was being watched, the man stopped shoveling food to his mouth and contemplated the big Indian standing at the edge of his campsite. "*Háu kola,*" he said placing the spoon on the plate and raising his hand.

Stone Eagle grunted, "*Háu kola.*" He stayed close to the bush at the edge of the creek so he could flee if he needed to. The man by the fire looked somehow familiar, but he didn't know why.

"You've been on the mountain?" the man asked tilting his head towards Bear Butte.

Stone Eagle nodded.

"Then you must be hungry." The man reached into a bag behind him and pulled out another plate. He spooned some steaming cornmeal from the pot sitting in front of him onto the plate and held it out towards Stone Eagle. "Did you find what you were searching for?"

Stone Eagle took the plate without answering, shoving his fingers into the mush and greedily pushing it into his mouth. In less than minute he was licking the plate clean.

"I'm searching too," the younger man said. "They say the mountain is close to the spirits of the Sioux. Did the spirits help you?"

Stone Eagle looked up from the plate and shook his head slowly.

"I'm Fire Brush of the Dakota Sioux, in Minnesota."

Stone Eagle carefully set the plate down by the fire. Out of the corner of his eye he measured the distance to the cover of the brush by the creek. Fire Brush continued to watch him.

"Are you Lakota?"

"I was." Stone Eagle's eyes drifted toward Bear Butte.

"Why aren't you living on the reservation? Where have you been?"

"Away," he said, returning his focus to the younger man. "I couldn't be Lakota anymore."

Fire Brush kicked at a rock in front of him. "I know what you mean. They sent me to the white man's school to stop being Sioux." He shrugged. "Who's an Indian, anyway? They took it from me. They took being an Indian from me."

Stone Eagle stared vacantly.

The sound of slow-moving hoof beats came from the road. Instinctively, Stone Eagle sprang to his feet, scrambled back to the stream bank and hid behind the chokecherry bushes. There wasn't time to do anything but lie flat. He could just see the camp through an open spot in the brush.

"Hey you, Indian!" a rough voice called.

From his hiding place, Stone Eagle heard the deep thud of the hooves as the horses approached. The two riders didn't look like cowboys. Neither one of them had the smooth cowboy way of sitting in a saddle and becoming part of the horse.

"Yes?" Fire Brush said, rising to stand in front of the little campfire.

The man on the left pointed at him. "You seen any other Injuns around here? We're lookin' for a big ol' buck named Stone Eagle." He pulled at the end of a long brown mustache framing his mouth.

"I'm here alone, to climb the mountain," Fire Brush said, nodding towards Bear Butte. "Here to visit the Sioux spirits."

The second man had a thick, black beard. He rode into the little clearing and around the fire pit, saying nothing. Stone Eagle watched him carefully as he leaned over to look at the campfire and stared at the plate he'd tossed aside. The man rode so close to the bushes that Stone Eagle could smell the big horse.

"So you ain't seen no other Injuns out here?" the first man said. He looked suspiciously at Fire Brush and spat a line of tobacco juice across the hard ground. "This here Stone Eagle is a big ol' buck."

"Why are you looking for him? What's he done?"

"Well, that's just none of your business, Injun." The cowboy smiled smugly but couldn't stop talking. "He's been mostly a harmless drunk a'hangin 'round Deadwood for years and then a few days ago he got caught stealin' outta the back of the Franklin. He threw ol' Jenkins right on the stove."

Stone Eagle had a disturbing memory of throwing the man away from him toward the stove. Most of that night was lost to him, but he remembered the howls of pain and the smell of burning flesh. He had only wanted a little food and the man had come at him with a knife.

"Goddamned worthless buck cut him too!"

Stone Eagle covered the blood stain on his sleeve with his hand.

"I haven't seen any Indians out here. I'm just here to climb the mountain."

The first man brought his horse a few steps closer to Fire Brush. "Well, you see him, you let us know an' nobody else. *Comprende?*" He leaned over his horse pointed at the Indian. "They wouldn't pay you no bounty on him anyway."

He turned the head of his horse and nodded to his silent partner. They slowly ambled up the bank and onto the road.

The sound of hooves on the hard scrabble faded and Stone Eagle slowly rolled into the open.

Fire Brush was packing the plates into a leather sack. "Looks like you got yourself some trouble. I don't want to be here when they come back for you."

Stone Eagle's voice rumbled, "Thank you for not telling them where I was."

"I have enough problems. I don't need any white men hanging around," he said as he stuffed gear into the bag. "It's time to get out of here."

Suddenly, a rifle shot cracked from behind him and a bullet thumped into the bank. They both dove for the ground as the sound of another shot filled the air. Hooves thundered toward them. "See, I told you there was a second plate," the man with the black beard yelled as he spurred on his big black horse.

"Don' kill 'im or we won't get no bounty," the other man shouted as he struggled to control his horse.

Stone Eagle rolled toward the little creek. Out of the corner of his eye he caught a glimpse of Fire Brush scrambling through the bushes and headed upstream. "Don't worry about that one," he heard the rough-voiced man shout. "Stone Eagle's got the bounty on him. We'll get the other one later." Stone Eagle dove forward, half running, half crawling, to get to the stream. The rough brambles tore at his face. He cleared the brush and burst into the stream. As he hit the icy water, his momentum pitched him forward. He fell face first in a blur of arms and splashes and cold water. His soaked clothing weighed him down as he fought for traction on the slick rocks. In a terrified race for escape he sloshed towards the other side of the narrow creek. The bright light of the sun sparkling on the water disoriented him. His head pounded and he struggled to catch his breath as he stretched his arms toward the opposite bank. A harsh blow hit the back of his head and the water rose to his face just before everything went black.

He opened his eyes to a silent world. Blurry rocks swam in front of his eyes and he was suddenly aware that was underwater. In his panic, he sucked in more water through his mouth. *Is this finally my time to die?* he thought.

His head was snapped back violently by a hand grasping his hair. Air hit his face and a wall of noise filled his ears. He coughed, struggling to regain his breath as rough hands dragged him forward and dropped him. He landed with his face planted in the rock and mud of the bank. A heavy weight crushed Stone Eagle's ribs as the man drove a knee into his back and yanked his arms behind him. Gravel crunched against his cheekbones. His head clouded in pain and he couldn't get air into his lungs. The weight left his back as suddenly as it had dropped on him. He rolled to his side and tried to suck in a breath. As he lifted his head from the gravel, a boot caught him in the ribs and rolled him over on his back. With his hands tied behind him, he flopped helplessly and the bright sun blinded him.

"Stay where you are, Injun!" the black-bearded man yelled at him. He was only a dark silhouette against the sun. "You son of a bitch, I'm soaked now!" The man grabbed him violently by his shirt and threw him higher up the bank, bouncing his head on the stones. Rolling to his side, Stone Eagle coughed out the water in his nose and mouth.

"Goddamn it, Jasper, get my horse before he bolts. You're the worst goddamn rider in the whole goddamn country."

"I'm tryin', damnit!" the other man shouted as another horse's hooves splashed through the creek. "Just keep hold o' that ol' buck!"

The black-bearded man stepped away from him, but Stone Eagle was too exhausted and beaten to move. "He's right there, damn it, get his bridle," the man yelled.

"I got 'im," the other voice said from up the bank. "I got 'im right he—Ahhh, crap!"

A loud thump came from up on the bank. "Jesus Christ, get off the ground and get the horses!" the black-bearded man said. He jumped up on the bank and a shower of gravel cascaded down on Stone Eagle's face. "They're both gonna bolt! Get off the goddamned ground and help me get 'em or we'll have to walk all the way back to Deadwood!"

Stone Eagle heard a rustle up the creek bank and the thud of boots running. He wiggled on his back, but couldn't move his arms.

A hand gripped his shoulder and rolled him to his side. He felt a knife slice at the leather thong on his wrists. Turning his head, he saw Fire Brush's face covered in sweat.

"Run, man," Fire Brush said, his jaw tight. "I got the short one's horse with a rock, but when they catch him, they'll be back, and mad as hell. Get outta here! Get out of the Hills! Do something. Go be Lakota."

Stone Eagle turned over and forced himself to his feet. Fire Brush shoved him upstream and Stone Eagle stumbled a few steps in the creek. He turned in time to see the younger man splashing downstream towards where the riders were chasing their horses.

Still trying to clear his head, Stone Eagle turned and stumbled along in the shallow water along the bank of the stream. He heard voices in the distance, but he never turned his head to look at them. A dry wash appeared on his left and he clawed his way up into it. He crawled under a big pile of tumbleweeds caught in a bend of the little wash. The sharp thorns tore at his skin and blood pounded in his head. Once he got in the middle, he curled himself into a little ball. He tried to control his breathing to stay as quiet as possible.

He remained hidden for the rest of the day. There was no sound other than the incessant buzzing of flies. He hated the image of himself cowering under the tumbleweeds. He wanted to be a warrior. He wanted to fight. He wanted to be Lakota. But he could do nothing but lie silently under the weeds like an animal.

When it was dark, he could leave, run and hide. He was disgusted with himself but could think of nothing else to do. There was nothing to drink and the spirits of Bear Butte had abandoned him.

He would go back to the Badlands. It was the only other place he knew. Maybe the spirits could find him there. Maybe he could be Lakota again.

Chapter Four

E VAN SCRAMBLED UP the last and steepest part of the ridge, feet pushing through the crust of the Badlands clay. It wrapped around his ankles, filling his boots. Streams of loose dirt and small rocks tumbled down the ridge with each step, sounding like a rush of heavy rain. With a final gasp, he heaved himself over the top, nose only inches from the ground. The sun had baked deep cracks into the ground, until it looked like the skin of an old, old man. It was rough on his hands and crackled under his feet as he rose to stand.

It was good to feel the sun on his face as he took in the panorama to the south. The crest was only three feet wide, but almost flat. He pushed the mop of sweaty hair out of his eyes and squinted against the bright light reflecting off the bleached ground.

Still gasping for air from the climb, he gazed across the valley below toward the Mystic Table, another mile to the west. That mile was a maze of steep hills, sharp spires and deep ravines. He could cover a mile on the flats of the prairie in no time, but he knew from experience that you couldn't get anywhere in a straight line through the Badlands.

He got a catch in his throat every time he came over the top of a ridge and saw the majesty of the Badlands spread out at his feet—and no other human being in sight. The maze of interlocking cuts and spires and the amazing shapes they created looked like chaos to some, but he knew how most of them locked together in an intricate web. While most people saw only the white-gray spires of a harsh, dry land, if they took the time to look closely they'd discover the intricate bands of color. One of his favorite sights was when the late afternoon sun hit the spires just right, and the bands of reds and yellows magically came to life, creating a glow all across the Badlands.

This was the one place he felt connected. In town, at school and sometimes even at home, he felt like a mildly unwelcome visitor. But here in this rugged land that nobody had any use for, he felt like he belonged. The raw power of the Badlands filled the air and he drew strength from it. He thought the ram must have also drawn on this power to have lived so long in such a strong and beautiful place.

"Jesus H. Christ! Do you have any idea where you're going?" a man's voice suddenly boomed from behind him. He turned from the sunlit vista and looked down the shaded north side of the ridge. His father, following his tracks, was nearing the steep last thirty feet of the climb.

"Up here, Pa," he said. "You can see the Table from here." He reached out a hand though his father was still several yards downslope.

James grumbled as he clawed his way up the steep incline, using their old Winchester hunting rifle as a walking stick. Evan winced. He'd wanted to carry the rifle through the rough terrain, but his father insisted on bearing it himself.

Finally, the big man crawled to the top of the saddle on all fours, ignoring his son's outstretched hand and filling the Winchester with more dust and dirt. He sat back on his haunches, his chest rattling audibly. Large semicircles of sweat stained his shirt beneath his arms.

Evan turned back to the view below them. "You see, Pa, these ravines all flow down toward the base of the Mystic Table." He pointed across the valley. "From the Table, the ram can climb up into any of the bowls at the end of these box canyons. See the way the spires surround that little flat area just a quarter-mile up there? You can even see a little bit of green grass."

James was still breathing heavily, but he struggled to his feet on the narrow ridgeline next to his son. He was only an inch or two taller than Evan now, though he weighed nearly twice as much. "If you think it'll be in the bowl, why don't we just walk up the valley and shoot it?" he asked.

"First of all, Pa, look at the ravine. It's steep and deep. Sometimes you can't even see the bottom. Sometimes it's so narrow you can't fit through. In the spring, the water makes new tunnels and cracks and sinkholes. And besides that, the ram would be able to see us." Evan was pointing at the prospect in front of them, but his father was looking in the opposite direction.

"Wouldn't we have it trapped in the box canyon then?" James said, brushing at the dust turned to mud on his sweaty forehead and pushing back his damp hair.

"You and I couldn't climb over those spires, but the ram would go right up the side. We need to cross the ridge above the bowl and wait for him. If he goes to the bowl to feed we may get a shot."

James spit as far as he could down the slope. "Jesus, I hate this godforsaken place! Are you sure there isn't a way to just put some food out for bait and shoot the bastard when he comes to eat?"

Evan let silence hang in the air. He still wasn't sure why they wanted to shoot the ram in the first place. It didn't make sense that everyone was so excited that the ram existed and then so focused on stalking him to extinction. Hunting with David was different. It was an adventure. It was just him and David and the Badlands. The guns and the animals were just a reason to be there.

"It looks like we'll need to follow this ridge across the top to that saddle, cut across the face of the spire and then come down the next ridge to get the best position," Evan finally said.

His father turned to face him. "You mean climb all the way up to that spire just to go down on the other side? It can't be more than half a mile from here. Why don't we just go straight across?"

Evan saw the impatience in his father's sweat and dirt-rimmed eyes. He wished he'd stuck to his refusal to guide him to the ram. In the end, he always seemed to do what his parents wanted.

"Pa, look at how steep it is on this side, and it's even worse on the other. It's even steeper than what we just climbed. You see that ledge below us? It probably drops straight down. And then there's the cracks worn into the ledge. Anyone who's been to the Badlands could tell you it's way too dangerous to try to cross here." He knew his insolent tone would make him angry but he couldn't stop himself.

His father flushed red and little red spiderwebs of blood vessels came to life around his face. "Just because you spend your time traipsing around out here like a goddamned Indian, instead of working in the store, doesn't mean you know more than I do. Let's not forget who's thirteen and who's the adult."

The volume of his voice increased with each syllable and echoed off the spires. "It's just stupid to climb clear up that ridge and all the way across, when we could cut most of the distance off by going straight over." He jabbed his finger into the air.

"Pa, I'm telling you we can't go down there," Evan said, frustration filling his voice. He could see that the top twenty feet down the ravine was on a steep but climbable grade, but he didn't know what was over the ledge. The wind and water that formed the Badlands may have cut deep cracks in the bedrock. In their explorations of the Badlands, he and David had come close to falling into deep crevices several times. Morgan told them if they fell in they'd join the ghosts of the Sioux Nation and never return.

"Damn it, Evan, I said we were going straight across and that's what we're going to do." James stomped his foot into the clay and brushed the dust off his pants. "I have a trophy to kill. You think you're a great guide. Now guide, damn it."

James sidestepped his way off the crest one foot at a time. Each step crumbled the hard crust, sending streams of small rocks noisily down the slope to gather at the lip of the ledge twenty feet below them.

Evan watched, hands on his hips, from the top of the ravine as his father's footsteps set the loose earth rushing down the slope. At school, at home, in the store, almost everywhere, he was told he didn't know how to do things. But in the Badlands, he knew what he was doing and he knew that trying to cross this ravine was the wrong thing to do. James held the Winchester high in the air with his right hand and used his left to balance on the slope.

"Come on, Pa, please. Let me help you back up here and we can go around," he yelled down the slope. He knew what the response would be.

"Evan," his father shouted, turning to look up at his son, "If I have to tell you once more—"

The shift of his body weight weakened his already tenuous hold. His left foot began sliding down the ravine. Instead of standing straight to regain traction, James instinctively leaned into slope and his whole body started sliding. He turned on his stomach and dropped the rifle as he clawed at the loose clay for something to stop him. The Winchester rattled down the ravine and went airborne as it hit the ledge.

"Pa!" Evan yelled as he skidded down the ravine on his butt, digging his heels into the clay.

"Goddamn it!" James bellowed as his legs went over the ledge and without any resistance, the rest of his body followed.

Evan reached the incline, forced his heels deep into the soft clay at the lip and leaned back. He spotted a small clump of native grass to his left and reached over to grab it. Its sharp blades cut into his fingers but provided enough resistance to stop his momentum.

He watched in horror as James careened down the steep slope in a pile of rubble and dust. Abruptly he stopped rolling, his arms outstretched and his body twisted at an odd angle.

"Pa, are you all right?" Evan yelled, carefully leaning over the ledge with his feet dug in deep for support. "Pa?"

"Ahhh, damn it. My leg's twisted into a crack and I can't move it," came James's response a moment later. He was lying on a second ledge and his leg was planted in the ground at an awkward angle. Just looking at it from the top of the ravine gave Evan a queasy stomach.

"It's gonna be okay, Pa. I'll be right down," Evan said, projecting a confidence he didn't feel. Slowly he worked his way down the steep slope, grasping at the sparse vegetation that speckled the face of the ravine. The sharp, tough blades of grass sliced tiny cuts into his fingers and soon his hands were covered with sticky blood and dirt. As he lost a foothold, a stream of loose gravel tumbled down the slope and splashed against his father, initiating an instant verbal outburst.

"Sorry, Pa," he yelled as he moved to right himself. James continued to sputter a steady stream of profanity, generally focusing on his pain, the Badlands, the trophy ram and the pace at which Evan was getting down the ravine.

Reaching the ledge, Evan could see that they'd been very lucky. The crack that caught James's leg at the knee flowed into a deeper opening. Had he continued to fall, he would have dropped straight down another twenty feet. Peering over the ledge made Evan shudder. It felt like he was being pulled over the ledge into thin air. He shook it off and turned to focus on his father.

After carefully planting his feet, Evan pulled on the neck of his father's coat, moving the big man slightly. James emitted a groan but removing the downward pressure relaxed the crack's grip on his leg.

"Now, Pa, I'm going to pull you all the way back so you can lean against the slope," he said. "Stay still so we don't start sliding again."

James mumbled an indistinguishable reply.

Once more digging in his heels, Evan gripped his father beneath his arms. Heaving up and arching his back, he pulled James on top of him up the slope. With a lurch they fell into a sitting position above the crack. James howled in pain as his knee twisted back to its correct position. Evan slipped out from beneath his father's body, careful not to let him slide back down the hill.

Evan stood and carefully anchored his feet and lifted James's injured leg by the knee, freeing it from the crack. James screamed and violently thrashed. Evan dropped down on top of him and held him in a bear hug to keep him from tossing them both over the ledge. He heard rocks falling and smashing against the ledge below them.

In a minute, James stopped moving. His chest heaved as he gasped for breath. "Get off me, boy! I can't breathe with you on me," he growled.

Evan raised his head, his face almost touching his father's. "We're right on the edge, Pa. If you're not careful, we'll both fall over," he said looking into James's eyes. He slowly rose and flopped down beside him.

"Now," he said, almost to himself, as he wiped the sweat off his forehead, "Morgan says when you're in a spot like this, the most important thing is to sit back and think before you stumble ahead and make things worse."

"I don't give a rat's ass what Morgan says. Just get me the hell out of here," James spat. He tried to rise, but the pressure on his injured knee sent him into another spasm of pain.

"Damn it, Pa," Evan said, more sharply than he had ever spoken to his father. "You're going to get both of us killed. Sit down, stay still, shut up and let me think."

James looked at him incredulously. "Why you—"

"I said shut up and let me think!" Evan cut him short. "I need to figure out how to get us out of here."

His father's mouth opened for a second and then closed with what looked like a great deal of self-control. After awhile he said quietly, "All right, big shot, you led us in here, you get us out. But you better hurry because it'll be dark soon."

Evan held an arm out in front of him and measured the distance between the sun and the horizon. "We've got almost an hour," he said, leaning toward James. "See, four fingers' worth."

James stared at his son for a good ten seconds and then turned away muttering to himself. There would be hell to pay when they got home, but Evan didn't have time to worry about it.

Look at the problem in pieces, he told himself. First he needed to find something to splint his father's leg. It must hurt bad the way he groaned, Evan figured. The next thing was to get off the steep ledge before dark. They'd fall if they tried to spend the night on it. Once they made it to level ground, he'd figure out how to get home.

There was no wood in sight, but the Winchester might work for a splint if he could find it. "Pa, I'm going to slide down and look for the rifle and scout a way out of here. Please don't move," he said, touching his father's shoulder and looking into his eyes. James nodded in response.

The crack that had trapped James's leg widened just below them, forming a deep cut into the side of the ravine. As he peered over the edge, Evan saw a rock formation about fifteen feet below that interrupted the sharp cut. If they could make it to the rock formation, they might be able to follow the narrow ledge and gradually reach the floor of the ravine.

Evan slid down into the crack. It quickly widened to three or four feet, just enough space for him to wedge his back against one wall and his feet against the other. By slowly walking down the crack, sliding his back against the wall, he could descend it like a chimney. He knew he could climb back up using both sides as leverage.

Not far down, he saw the old Winchester to his left, caught on a small outcropping. Continuing to wedge his back against the crack, he reached over and got two fingers on the barrel. He pulled it loose and was able to catch it before it fell to the bottom of the ravine.

He grimaced in disgust at the dirt and dust that filled the gun. Even with a thorough cleaning it might never shoot again.

Holding the rifle in one hand and pushing against the wall with the other, he inched his way up, sliding his back against one wall of the crack and then repositioning his feet against the opposite wall. It was a laborious climb, but he finally cleared the ten feet to the top. "Pa, grab the gun," he said as he thrust it through the crack. James grunted as he pulled the rifle up. Free from his burden, Evan hoisted himself up onto the ledge. He sat, dangling his feet over the crack, and struggled to catch his breath.

"Well," James said ,shaking dust from the rifle, "What're we going to do with this? And how're you going to get me out of here?"

Weary and silent, Evan stared out over the landscape.

Part of him wanted to be the little boy who just did what he was told. He wanted his father to decide what to do. The other part knew that if they were going to get off this slope, he would have to be the one to figure out a plan. With a surge of determination, he pulled off his shirt and began ripping it into long wide strips. The sharp sound of tearing echoed in the silence of the Badlands.

"Your mother will kill you for ruining that shirt," his father said absently as Evan continued to rip..

He leaned over James's injured leg and gently straightened it. James twitched, his face contorted in pain. "I'm going to use the rifle as a splint for your leg," Evan told him. "There's no wood around and the gun's dirty and ruined anyway."

He looked over his shoulder up the ravine. It would be a thirty- or forty-foot climb through loose rock to the top. He could make it but it was too steep for his father, even if his leg wasn't hurt. If he went himself, it would take hours to climb the slope and bring back help. James couldn't stay on the ledge after dark. Climbing down the crack was the only way to get them both out.

"We can't make it back up the hill and we can't say here all night," he said as he tied the rifle to James's leg with the cloth strips. "We're down to about half an hour of daylight. We're going to have to drop through this crack. About fifteen feet down there's a rock ledge we can follow to the floor of the ravine. We can spend the night there and figure out how to get out in the morning." He moved his father's leg back and forth gently to test the splint.

"Spend the night?" James sputtered. "I'm not going to sleep out in this hell hole. I want—"

"Damn it, Pa!" Evan broke in sharply. "Don't you understand we're in a fix? Your knee is so twisted you can't walk and we're thirty feet above the wash. If we fall we'll probably both die. Hell, we'll be lucky to get to the bottom alive before dark, so stop worrying about sleeping in a goddamned bed!"

James looked startled. Evan had never uttered a swear word around his father before.

"Listen to me, Pa." Evan turned to look intently into his face. "This is going to be hard and I need you to do exactly what I say. I know you're hurt, but you gotta listen."

James responded to his earnest look and nodded.

"Here's what we'll do," Evan said in a clear, precise voice. "I'm going to climb down a few feet, brace myself and then call for you. You slide down and give me your good leg. You'll have to press your hands against the sides of the crack to hold yourself up. I'll hold your good leg while you put weight on it and your bad leg can dangle off the edge. You can lower yourself by moving your hands a little bit at a time. Understand?" James nodded.

He continued. "When you get down to me you'll need to hold yourself up by bracing your arms to the sides while I climb down a little further and then we'll do it again."

"Evan, that won't work," James said in a voice just above a whisper. "You can't hold my weight and I can't—"

"It's the only way, I'm telling you. I thought of all the others. This is it. We're running out of daylight. You ready?" Evan's eyes focused fiercely on his father.

James took a deep breath and nodded.

Evan's gaze softened. "This will work. Now don't move until I tell you to."

He lowered himself down into the crack. The rough clay scratched his stomach as he kicked his legs until he could get a toe hold on the wall. He slid down as deliberately as possible using his hands and feet against the sides. With his back against one wall and feet on the other, he supported his weight by extending his legs. Taking a deep breath he said, "Okay, Pa, lower your feet first and support yourself with your hands."

James rolled over and dangled his bad leg, now splinted with the rifle. As he slid into the crack, a heavy rain of clay poured down beneath him, spattering Evan's face and chest. He squawked and sputtered, spitting out dirt. As he tried to shake the dust and gravel off his face, his foot slipped and he felt his body slipping down into the crack. His stomach burned on the verge of panic as he scrambled to anchor his feet before he slid down the crack.

"Evan! Evan, are you okay?" James shouted, unable to look down, his legs dangling into the crack.

"*Pttttuuuuu* . . . Yeah, I'm fine," Evan said, shaking the dirt out of his face as he repositioned himself. That had been far too close. *Breathe, breathe,* he told himself. He reached up and held the boot on his father's good leg. "Now lower yourself slowly. I have your leg."

James slid into the crack, placing increasing weight on the good leg his son was holding while he dangled his injured leg in the air. Evan brought the leg to his chest and then stomach, holding tight with both hands. He pressed his legs even harder into the wall to support the weight. He felt the clay digging into his back and his feet slipping. Out of the corner of his eye he watched the gravel falling noisily beneath them. A wave of dizziness washed over him as he felt gravity trying to pull him through the crack. He flexed his legs as tightly as he could to hold his own weight and his father's. It felt like the weight of the world was on the pit of his stomach.

When most of James's weight was on him, Evan said in a tightly controlled voice, "Okay, now press your hands against the sides to support yourself and I'll move lower down." James grunted and complied.

The pressure lightened on the center of Evan's stomach. He slowly walked his feet lower and slid down the wall on his back until he could just reach his father's boot again. "Come on down," he said, breathing heavily and ignoring the painful scrapes on his barely clad back. He resolved not to look down again until he had to.

James gasped as he lowered himself, straining his arms against the wall of the crack. A rain of dirt and pebbles fell into Evan's face and chest again, but not as heavy as the first time. Slowly, James transferred his weight to his son until he heard Evan mutter through clenched teeth, "Okay, one more time."

They completed the maneuver for the last time with much more coordination. Evan dropped to stand on the rock ledge, grabbing his father's good leg and slowly lowering him to stand beside him. James unconsciously leaned on his bad leg. He winced and staggered, pulling both of them toward lip of the ledge. Evan felt another wave of dizziness as the floor of the ravine loomed below. He grabbed his father's shirt with both hands and threw himself back against the wall.

Together, they slid to a sitting position on the lower rock ledge. There were deep lines of pain and fatigue in his father's face. Small trails of sweat ran down Evan's neck into the remains of his torn and dirty shirt. The sweat stung when it hit the scrapes on his back. As they sat in silent relief, the rasping of their labored breathing was the only sound in the Badlands. They could already smell the cool, clean night air filling the darkening ravine.

From the corner of his eye, Evan thought he saw movement at the top of the next ridge. He watched intently, but couldn't make out anything for certain. It wasn't as if they could hunt the sheep now, anyway.

"I think, if we move slowly, you should be able to just slide along this ledge to get down to the floor," he told his father.

James sat with his shoulders slumped and nodded without looking up.

With one arm around Evan's shoulders and his bad leg dangling, he slid along the ledge as it angled toward the ground. When they were only five feet or so from the bottom of the ravine, Evan dropped down, landing steadily on his feet. James slowly lowered himself into Evan's arms and eased his way to the ground.

They stood arm-in-arm leaning against the wall as they surveyed the ravine. The floor was about ten feet wide and almost perfectly flat. It was covered with hard, silty sand and a few scrub sage plants.

High above them, the tops of the spires reflected the gold of the setting sun. They glowed with bright bands of pinks and reds, and from the shadows of the wash they looked like grand castles.

"Will we have a fire?" James asked.

"I don't think there's time to find any wood before it gets dark. Besides, I didn't bring any matches. Did you?"

His father sighed deeply and shook his head. "You're the expert out here."

Evan wasn't sure if he was being sarcastic or not. "How's your leg, Pa?"

"Hurts like hell," he said. He paused and then added, "Using the rifle for a splint was a good idea. I don't know how I would have gotten down otherwise."

Evan was surprised and a little uncomfortable with the praise. "Thanks," he muttered and busied himself brushing the dirt from his pants.

"What're we going to do tomorrow?" James asked as he carefully repositioned his splinted leg on the hard ground.

"Well, I know you won't be able to walk out, especially from here," Evan said as he tossed a rock at a plant across the wash. "I'll get us out somehow, don't worry."

James looked at his son a long time. "I know you will," he said. He rolled over and curled his good leg under him.

Evan leaned his head back against the wall of the ravine and let the stillness of the Badlands wash over him. He looked over at his sleeping father and sighed. Then he curled up next to him. "It'll be all right, Pa," he whispered.

Chapter Five

MORNING PENETRATES THE SHADOWS in the deep ravines of the Badlands slowly. The sun was well overhead when the peaceful calls of the meadowlarks were interrupted by a rough voice.

"Mornin', boys. Get too drunk to come home last night?"

"Morgan!" Evan yelled sitting up with his back to the bank. "Morgan, how did you find us?" Relief washed over him as the load of responsibility left his shoulders. The cowboy was at the bend of the wash, bathed in the rays of the morning sun, sitting easily on old Blue. His crossed arms rested in front of him on the saddle horn and a slight smile appeared among the deep lines on his weathered face.

"Little bird told me you boys had a bit of trouble," he drawled, pushing his hat up on his forehead.

"Morgan!" James grunted as he rolled over. He let out a groan of pain as he moved his leg. "Morgan, thank God you're here. We didn't know what we were going to do."

The old rancher regarded the two men sprawled in the dust of the wash. "Looks to me like you got things in pretty good order," he drawled, shading his eyes with a gloved hand and gazing up at ledge above them absently.

"Morgan," James said, "how're you going to get us out of here? I don't think I can walk. Shall I ride Blue?"

Morgan pushed his hat up higher on his forehead, and his blue eyes appeared beneath the brim as he took out his gold watch. "Dunno." He looked up and turned to Evan. "Evan, what do you think we should do?"

James looked at his son like he had forgotten he was there. Evan's eyes lit up and he started talking quickly. "Well, I don't think Pa will be able to ride through the rough spots where the washes come together." He interlocked his fingers. "I was thinking of rigging up a travois so I could pull him out. With Blue here, he could pull it."

"A travois?" James asked, looking at Morgan. "What's that?"

"It's kind of an Indian wagon without wheels," Evan answered quickly before Morgan had time to reply. He held out three fingers and put a finger from his other hand another across them.

Morgan spit once into the wash and nodded his head slowly. "Good idea, boy. Probably the only way to get him out of here." Evan smiled for the first time since they had entered the Badlands the day before.

"I saw a dead scrub pine down the way," Morgan said sliding off his horse. "Evan, you take Blue down there and see if you can get some poles, if you want. There's a little rope in the saddle bags."

Evan jumped to his feet and took the reins from Morgan. "How should I tie it?"

Morgan squinted and shook his head. "You'd know better than I would. However you think will work."

Evan raced over to Blue and practically leaped into the saddle. His feet didn't reach the stirrups, but he knew he could stay up on the reliable old mount. "See you in a little bit," he said enthusiastically. He paused and looked back over his shoulder at his father. "Don't move that leg, Pa." Then he turned back, shook the reins once and headed Blue down the wash.

James looked after Evan and shook his head. "Morgan, I'm so glad you're here. Lost and hurt in the Badlands with only the boy. I was a goner."

The old cowboy stood in the middle of the wash with his thumbs hooked in his pants pockets. "By the look of things, that boy did more for you than I ever could'a." Morgan gazed up at the tops of the spires above, and then back at Warner. "From what I hear, what he did gettin' you down here off that wall was something that many a grown man wouldn't a tried. You oughtta be right proud of him."

"Whaddyou mean, 'What you hear?' There somebody else out here?" James asked, looking around them.

Morgan seemed not to hear Warner's question, but tilted his head back to look up at the wall of the ravine. "What the hell were you doing up there, anyway?"

James hesitated and looked down. "It was, uh, too long of a way to go around so we decided to cut across." He groaned softly as he shifted around, trying to make his injured leg hurt less.

"Bad choice." Morgan spat on the ground and kicked dirt from the wash over it with the heel of his boot. He ambled over to where James sat in the shrinking shade of the canyon wall and tossed him a piece of jerky. While James greedily tore into the dried beef, Morgan took a swig of water and handed the canteen to him, saying, "Save some for the boy."

In a few minutes Evan appeared on foot, leading Blue. The ends of three gnarled gray pieces of scrub pine were tied to the saddle and dragging behind.

"You think this will work, Morgan?" Evan asked as soon as they were in sight.

Morgan examined the travois and nodded his head in approval. "Good idea threadin' the rope through there like that," he said, tossing Evan his well-worn leather bag. "Have a piece of jerky and some water 'fore we head outta here."

Evan smiled and wiped the sweat from his forehead. The morning sun was quickly warming the ravine. "So, Morgan, how did you find us?" he asked, sitting down next to the men. "You must'a been riding all night."

Without answering, Morgan scanned the top of the spire on the other side of the ravine. Evan followed his gaze up to the horizon. He gasped as he saw the silhouette of a man on a horse in one of the shadows of the spire. "Morgan . . ." He pointed and looked back over at the old cowboy.

Morgan had raised an arm just over his head and seemed to Evan to make a small gesture with his hand. Evan looked back to the horizon in time to see the man in the shadow of the spire turn his horse and vanish over the edge of the ravine. When Evan looked back at Morgan, the rancher gave him a quick, hard stare with his eyebrows knitted down low over his eyes that seemed to tell Evan to keep what he saw to himself.

James looked up from tearing at the jerky. "What're you waving at?" he said with his mouth full.

Morgan cocked his head at Evan and gave him a hard look as he lowered his arm. "Not a thing," he said to James. "Not a damn thing."

The old cowboy grunted and pulled himself to his feet. He looked down at Evan and winked. "Well, boss, when do we go?" he asked, pulling out his watch.

Evan sat a little straighter and said in an authoritative voice. "Help me get Pa onto the travois. You and I'll walk old Blue."

He and Morgan each took an arm and they pulled the big man onto the travois. Evan had left part of the rope loose so he could put a length across his father's chest and tie him securely.

They walked on either side of Blue, dragging the travois down the smooth sand of the wash. James grumbled as he was loaded on the travois, but then rode silently for the most part. Evan looked back at the grooves they etched in the sand of the wash and their footprints trailing on either side.

Satisfied that the system was working, Evan looked at Morgan across the horse's withers. "How come you never told me you were at Wounded Knee before the other night?" he asked.

Morgan was walking along silently with a slight limp and kept his head tilted to the side to keep the sun out of his face. "Didn't see why you needed to know," he said.

They walked on for a while with only their footsteps and the scratching of the travois on the hard ground interrupting the silence of the Badlands. "What did happen there, Morgan?" Evan asked finally. "At Wounded Knee, I mean? Nobody ever says much about it."

They walked on for several more minutes, scrambled up two steep embankments and reached another flat area with the question lingering in the warm morning air. Sweat ran in tiny droplets down Evan's face and stung his eyes. He looked back. His father looked to be asleep on the travois. Judging from that, Evan figured his travois had gotten James up the steep hillsides of the ravine without much pain to his knee.

Morgan continued to hold Blue's reins in a leather-gloved hand. The cowboy was moving noticeably slower now and limping more. Evan had never thought of Morgan as any particular age, but right now he looked old.

"Should we rest a little, Morgan?" Evan asked, as he made a show of wiping his brow. "That last climb really took it out of me."

Morgan trudged on without looking up. Then, he started talking. "We had thought we was going to get a nice warm Christmas at Fort Sully. Hadn't done much but march around and show off for years. Wasn't much real soldierin' left to do by 1890. I was lookin' to muster out when my hitch was up and maybe go back home to Ohio."

He pulled his hat even lower over his brow to block the sun and kept walking, his eyes focused on the ground in front of him. Evan rested a hand against Blue and felt the long, hard muscles in the horse's chest. He walked with one eye on the ground in front and one watching Morgan. He couldn't help but notice the shadows the sun cast on the lines in Morgan's face.

"Then we started hearin' about a buncha' Indians down in Nevada or Arizona gettin' all churned up about a Ghost Dance. They said that after they danced awhile, the white man's bullets couldn't kill them. They would just hit their Ghost Dance shirt and fall off," he said, shaking his head. "Damned fools.

"Buncha' Lakota went down to see about this Ghost Dance and got all excited about it. Some folks said they were gonna to start a whole new uprising like in '62 or '77. They said that the whole bunch of 'em were going to the Stronghold in the Badlands and then they was gonna come out fightin'.

"Well, that got the brass all excited. They decided to round up the leaders before they could get all banded together. The thought of the tribes working together like they was at Little Big Horn scared the hell outta 'em. Somebody tried to bring ol' Sitting Bull in to jail up in North Dakota and ended up killin' him. Dumb bastards. Wasn't like Sitting Bull wanted another fight. He'd been doin' shows back East with Bill Cody, for God's sake. Just warn't no warriorin' left in him.

"After they killed Sittin' Bull, Big Foot lit out of there with his bunch headed to the Stronghold, here in the Badlands. We got sent out to stop 'em. The boys were ready for a good old fashioned Indian fight. Have to say, I'd been pretty bored myself." Morgan kicked at a rock and it went flying.

"So did you go hunting the Indians?" Evan asked. "Were you a scout?"

"Pshaww . . . you read too many of those damned dime novels," Morgan said, wiping his mouth with the back of his leather glove. "I was just a grunt soldier." He patted Blue on the nose. "And huntin' Indians was just ridin' where the officers told us. Up and down those damned hills. It was cold . . . bitter cold and windy. I 'bout froze to the saddle of that old nag I was ridin'." He grunted as they scrambled up another small embankment. As soon as they hit the flat top, he started back into his tale.

"We finally caught up to old Big Foot's bunch on the Wounded Knee Creek, about twenty miles from the Stronghold. Hell, I don't know if there ever was any Injuns up there. It sure as hell ain't no place to spend the winter."

Evan moved in front of Blue so he could hear Morgan better. In an excited voice he asked, "Was it a fierce battle when you caught 'em, Morgan?"

Morgan stopped walking and looked at the ground in front of him, lost in memory for a moment. He shook his head slowly and raised his eyes to meet Evan's.

"Naw, it was more like they were too tired and cold to go any further and we was too cold to keep chasin' 'em. Big Foot had about three hundred with him, 'bout half were women and kids. The old man himself was sick as a dog. They were camped down in the draw and we set up around them. Not a shot was fired. Night comin' on. We all just wanted to warm up and rest up and then get back to a nice warm barracks.

"But it was so damned cold none of us slept worth a damn. They told us to set up on the top of the draw with guns ready. They had me up on one of the little hills with one of our Hotchkisses."

"What's a Hotchkiss?" Evan asked, not wanting to interrupt but unable to restrain himself. He

Morgan resumed walking, shuffling his worn boots in the dry clay.

"It's kinda like eight guns wrapped into one. It could fire about thirty shots a minute. It was a heavy beast and you couldn't aim it worth a damn but it could throw a lotta lead."

"Did you shoot it?" Evan's eyes widened as he moved back to his place along Blue's side.

"It took two of us to shoot the damn noisy thing. And we had four of those big bastards on the hillsides covering both the ends of the draw and the camp itself."

"Then what happened?" Evan asked in a hushed voice, peering across the horse's back to see Morgan's face. He looked old and tired, older and more tired than Evan had ever seen him. It was as if every word of the story hurt him a little more.

"In the mornin' the officers and the Indians started talking down by the Indian camp. We couldn't see much up on the hills but it looked like they were trying to get the Indians to give up their guns. Damn fool officers were mixed in with the Indians. There was a little pile o' guns started and we all thought that we missed another big Indian fight.

"It was cold and crisp in the morning air and sound carried forever. Your breath hung right in front of your face like a cloud. It was gittin' plenty warm down by the camp where the guns were bein' stacked. We could hear all sorts of yellin' in English and Indian.

"Outta nowhere, a shot rang out, echoing through the valley. Everybody froze stock-still and looked around to see where it come from. Then all hell broke loose."

"Who fired the shot, Morgan?" Evan asked, trying to see Morgan's eyes under his hat brim. "Was it a soldier or an Indian?"

Morgan turned and looked at the boy with a grave expression that conveyed a deep, inner uncertainty. "I honestly don't know. I don't think anybody does for sure."

"What happened next, Morgan?" Evan asked. Somehow, Morgan's pace had increased and Evan found himself having to skip every few steps to keep up with the man's longer stride. "What did you do?"

Morgan stopped suddenly and was silent for a long time. "What happened next was that there was a buncha' dead Indians, a few dead soldiers, and nothin's ever been the same."

"But what was the fight like, Morg?" Evan persisted. "Did'ja kill anybody?"

Morgan turned rapidly on Evan. His blue eyes were now sharp and cold, colder than Evan'd ever seen them. "One thing you gotta learn, boy. Never ask somebody if they killed a man. If it's right to tell you, they will. Now hand me that canteen of water. I'm all talked out."

Evan tossed the canteen over to Morgan. The last five minutes had been the most he'd ever heard Morgan talk. But he still didn't know what happened or what part Morgan played. It didn't sound like the dime novels at all.

When the old cowboy finished his drink, he hung the canteen back on Blue's pommel and they walked in silence.

Finally, Evan couldn't stand the quiet any longer. He looked across the horse's nose to Morgan. "So who was that on the other side of the ravine, Morgan? I've never seen Indians out here in the Badlands."

Morgan's voice had now lost the hard edge of a moment ago. "You'll never see him if he don't want to be seen." Morgan paused, and added, "He saw you, all right. I hadn't heard him talk in years but he said the way you got your pa through the crack out there was something."

Evan felt his chest swell. "So who was it?"

"Just someone I know."

Evan had a sudden inspiration. "There *are* Indians out here, Morgan! The ghost Indians they talk about."

Morgan didn't say anything for a long time. He looked sternly at Evan. "Let's get you boys home. We've done wasted too much time talking already."

Chapter Six

STONE EAGLE HADN'T SEEN the Good River—that the *Wasicus* called Cheyenne—for years. It wound like a fat silver snake through the prairie bluffs. The water was milky white, full of sediment from rain in the mountains. Though it looked calm, there were white ripples around the pilings of the railroad bridge indicating a substantial current. The river was so full it lapped at the ties.

He watched the bridge from the top of the little bluff. A man and a woman were camped on the other side of the river with a five- or six-year-old boy and an infant. A bedroll extended from beneath an old push cart piled high with household items.

"I'm telling you, they probably won't even notice us on the bridge," a voice said from behind him.

Stone Eagle kept staring straight ahead. He liked watching the little family. They had been three hours and he hadn't moved.

Fire Brush climbed up beside him again. He had been back and forth several times.

"If you want to go, leave me alone," Stone Eagle said, his eyes still fixed on the family. A couple of days after evading the bounty hunters, the younger man had caught up to him again. He never said where he was going or why he was following him, but just fell into step.

"I told you, I don't have any place to go." Fire Brush pulled a strand of hair back from his face. "You need me to keep you out of trouble."

"Hrmphf," Stone Eagle grumbled. "Nobody asked you for help."

"How far is it to the Badlands after we cross the river?"

"About a day."

"Let's cross the rail bridge before the river gets any higher." Fire Brush fidgeted.

Stone Eagle knew he was right. The homesteader, his young wife and two young children posed no threat to them. Even if they saw them crossing the bridge, it was more than ten miles to Wall, where any authorities were located. There was no reason to suspect two Indian men of anything anyway.

But he enjoyed watching them. The man was in his late twenties or early thirties and his wife was about the same. They were huddled close to the little fire, bent over the bundled-up baby. The boy had wandered to the edge of the camp and was throwing stones into the swirling river. He was small but easily climbed the bank and scrambled onto the railroad bridge, jumping from tie to tie. Stone Eagle wanted to call out and warn the parents to watch their son. He turned to look at Fire Brush, who was back at the fire, rummaging impatiently in his bag.

Out of the corner of his eye he sensed movement and saw a splash of whitewater just below the bridge. A faint call rose from the noise of the rushing river. The boy wasn't on the bridge any longer.

A small arm rose out of the water ten feet downstream from the bridge. The father and mother were still huddled around the fire.

As a small white face briefly emerged from the current, Stone Eagle's stomach burned with energy that flowed out to his limbs. Before he knew what he was doing, he was running down the steep bank, his feet sinking into the sand.

"Stone Eagle! What are you doing?" Fire Brush's voice was a far off echo.

He was knee deep into the current before he even felt how cold the water was. He lunged headfirst and everything went silent. The powerful current rushed him along, swirling around his body.

Raising his head, he took a breath of air and tried to swim toward where he thought the boy should be. There was no sign of the boy and the rushing water pulled him back under. His soaked clothes were heavy, dragging down his arms and legs.

He tried to raise his head again for air and to look for the boy, but the current was too fast. He spread his arms and pushed upward against the onrushing water. His hand hit something soft. Instinctively, his fingers closed around it and gripped tightly. He'd found the boy, or rather, the boy had found him.

Pulling hard on the boy's shirt, Stone Eagle hauled him toward the surface, forcing his own body down. One foot hit the sandy bottom of the river and he pushed upward as hard as he could.

His head broke the surface and he lifted the boy clear of the water for a moment, but slipped back under again. He was shivering with cold and his strength was flagging quickly. In the moment he was above water he saw the current had moved them closer to the shore. He went down again, to get his feet against the bottom, and felt the comforting crunch of sand. He pushed up hard and thrust himself toward the shore.

The swiftly running water had pushed them downstream. The boy's body flopped lifelessly in the current and it was a struggle to maintain his grip. With another lunge against the sandy bottom, Stone Eagle got his head and shoulders above the surface and saw how the river bent hard to the left. They were on the outside of the bow on the right side where the water ran slower. He pulled them out of the main current and crawled toward the shore, still grasping the boy by the shirt.

The current had built a small sandbar against the outside bend of the turn. He pulled the boy onto the sandbar and collapsed, gasping for air, his feet still in the water. He coughed and felt the water that he'd swallowed churning in his stomach and lungs. A retch clamped his stomach and he threw up violently into the sand. He lay there, too spent to move.

The boy's body lay sprawled across the sandbar above him, unmoving. Stone Eagle wanted to get up to help, but he couldn't make his body move.

"Caleb, Caleb!" a man's voice rolled down from the top of the bank.

He felt more than saw the boy's father drop down beside the prone body. "Caleb, wake up!" the man cried, his voice betraying his panic.

"My God, my God, Caleb!" The man was weeping and rocking the boy back and forth.

"Move away and lay the boy flat," an authoritative voice called out. Stone Eagle rolled to his side and saw Fire Brush running down the bank.

"It's my son, he's dead," the man wailed.

"Lay him flat," Fire Brush said in a commanding voice as he reached them. "Raise his arms over his head."

Fire Brush knelt and put his hands on the boy's chest. The boy's father was kneeling above the boy's head, holding his arms.

"That's right, keep his arms spread wide and put his elbows to the ground," Fire Brush directed. He was leaning over the boy, pressing on his torso.

"Now, bring the arms together slowly and press them to his chest."

Suddenly, the little boy coughed. He coughed again, spitting up water. He started crying between gasps for air. As his lungs filled with air, he found his voice and cried harder.

"He'll be all right now," Fire Brush said in a remarkably calm voice.

"What did you do—to make him breathe, I mean?" the father said, holding the wailing boy to his chest. "Was it some Indian trick?"

Fire Brush laughed. "No, that was the Silvester Method of Resuscitation, as taught by Princeton's finest."

He placed his hand on Stone Eagle's arm and helped him up. "I'm afraid my friend and I need to get back on the road."

"You saved his life, both of you," the man said. "How did you know what to do?"

Fire Brush smiled. "They wanted me to be the new Charles Easton. 'Brilliant Indian Doctor,' emphasis on 'Indian.' And only fit to treat Indians."

The homesteader looked like he was trying to come to terms with the events of the last few minutes. He didn't even know any Indians and these two had just saved his son's life. They didn't look or talk like Indians were supposed to. "Well, thank you. What can I do to repay you?"

Stone Eagle groaned as he staggered to his feet. Rivulets of water ran from his clothing. He gazed at the boy, huddled against his father's chest, sobbing, and Fire Brush led him up the bank.

Fire Brush answered the man's question, "If anyone asks if you've seen a big Indian man come this way," Fire Brush said over his shoulder, "You didn't see anyone."

The man nodded silently and held his son's head close to his chest.

"What do you think you were doing?" Fire Brush said as they trudged up the opposite bank and out of earshot of the man. "You risk your life for a white boy?"

"No man should ever have to lose a son," Stone Eagle replied, his dark eyes fixed on Fire Brush's angry face. "How did you know how to make him breathe again?"

"The white man's medical school is good for something, I guess," the young man said. "Stay here while I get my bag. I left it on the road after I crossed the rail bridge. We'd better get away from the railroad so we don't run into any bounty hunters."

Stone Eagle rested by the side of the road. His lungs burned from all the water he'd swallowed, but otherwise he was unhurt. He wasn't sure why he'd gone in the water after the boy, but was glad he had.

When Fire Brush returned they made their way along one of the old wagon tracks that ran parallel to the rail line.

"So, are you going to tell me why you dove into a river for a white boy?" he asked.

"I had a son once. No man should ever lose a son."

"You had a son? How did you lose him?"

The big man turned his whole body to face Fire Brush. "Nobody asked you to come," he said.

Then he turned and continued on his way toward the Badlands.

Chapter Seven

FROM THE TOP OF THE PASS, David made out at least ten camps on the road running from the rail station in Murdo to the town of Interior. Most of the men hunting the sheep apparently wanted to stay near town rather than in the isolation of the Badlands. The camps ranged from single white army tents to a group of four large canvas tents. He assumed those belonged to the Englishman, Colonel Lauper. Mrs. Blake had delayed them only one day in Murdo—"to see a few people"—which meant that the extensive Lauper camp had gone up very quickly. He wondered if they'd found a guide yet.

The dream had come back to him last night. The voice talked to him in Lakota again and he knew that he understood it in the dream, though it meant nothing to him now. Instead of coming out of empty space, this time the voice seemed to swirl toward him from behind dark, shadowy shapes. He felt the shapes more than saw them. Although it made no sense in waking life, in his dream they felt like the spires of the Badlands.

The wagon lurched dramatically and Mrs. Blake shot her husband an angry look. With Edmund driving the wagon, Amanda in the middle and David on the outside, the Blakes were wedged uncomfortably into the front seat. Amanda would not hear of David riding in the back seat and she certainly wasn't going to. He didn't remember so many ruts in the road, but then, he had been living with city streets for two years.

In fact, many things had changed since he left. Mr. and Mrs. Blake looked at him differently more eye-to-eye. The people in Murdo looked at him differently as well. Before he left he was a curiosity, an Indian boy trying to act grown up and white. Now they were cautious around him and avoided looking into his eyes. It had been a long time since he felt like an Indian but it was clear that in this part of the country, people first saw the Indian and then looked at the man.

A dark green line of cottonwood trees came into view, running through Interior and down the dry creek to the south. To their right, the stark spires of the Badlands rose abruptly from the flat plains.

The town of Interior consisted of about thirty buildings clustered around the main road, although not in a uniform row. To David, they looked exactly the same as he remembered, except maybe dirtier and dingier. He couldn't remember a time when they were all occupied, and, from the way they looked, many of them were vacant now. He couldn't tell if the town had fallen further into disrepair or if he had merely forgotten how bad it always looked.

After passing through the tent city of the hunters, they drove right past the combination Land Office and residence where the Blakes lived.

It was the Indian reservation that had brought Amanda and Edmund to the plains of Dakota. Amanda pestered her influential brother-in-law to get Edmund an appointment as an assistant Indian agent. Even remote Dakota was better than living with Edmund's parents on the pig farm in Ohio.

In the volatile aftermath of Wounded Knee, Edmund had exhibited two qualities that set him apart from most federal employees: he was basically honest and had no ambitions. As far as the bureaucrats in Washington were concerned, silence was success, and they were more than willing to leave him alone. Much to Amanda's disappointment, Edmund would stay in Dakota.

When the Homestead Act brought an invasion of poor farmers to the area, all desperate for free land, Amanda used her connections to get Edmund out of the reservation and appointed to manage the Land Office for the area. He was well suited for administering bureaucracy quietly.

It was Mrs. Blake who determined they wouldn't stop at their house right away. "We'll just get right down to the store to show you off, David. Everyone will be so surprised at how much you've grown up," she said, unnecessarily smoothing down his hair.

"Yes ma'am," he said automatically. In his mind he heard her add ". . . and become civilized." Back East, he fit in when he walked down the street. Out here, he was like a circus act. *See the educated Indian!* He would play along—that's what he did best.

He slapped at the dust on the leg of his new suit. It had seemed rather silly to buy a new suit when they got off the train in Murdo just to wear back to Interior. David had thought his Pierceson School suit was just fine, but Mrs. Blake had insisted, saying, "It is important that the ruffians in town know how successful people dress."

When David looked to Mr. Blake for support, Edmund had just nodded his head in agreement, as he always did. David had never seen Mr. Blake directly disagree with his wife. In fact, he had never seen anyone else disagree with her either, at least not for very long.

There were more people milling about the main street than David had ever seen at one time. Mrs. Blake ran her hand over his hair one last time to make sure it was all in place. With the amount of oil she had put on it that morning, a tornado couldn't have mussed it.

They came to the Johnsons's shabby house on the edge of town. Like most of the buildings in Interior, it had been whitewashed sometime in the past, but the grayish-brown wood underneath was fighting to the surface in long streaks on every plank. The Johnsons were unloading supplies from their buckboard. Levi Johnson was a mountain of a man with a sunburnt face, large red beard, big gut and skinny legs. His daughter, Emily, almost David's age, stood next to her father swinging her skirts. Emily had always been a know-it-all. He smiled at at her and waved absently. He remembered that she had a screechy voice and was always tattling on the boys. Every time Mrs. Blake asked a question in lessons, Emily's hand shot up in the air waving for attention. In the back of the room, Evan would roll his eyes and make owl sounds to David in the row next to him.

However, the blonde pigtails and stick legs were gone now. Even in her formless calico dress it was clear to David that Emily was growing up. He noticed the little laugh crinkles around her green eyes for the first time. She giggled and waved back. "Hi, David." The voice was still screechy, but somehow it was considerably less annoying coming from a girl who was becoming an attractive young woman.

Mrs. Johnson, a short woman shaped like a tumbleweed with arms, legs and a head attached, stood next to Emily and raised her small chin at the wagon. Mrs. Blake waved at her. "Oh Gloria, you will have to come over this evening to visit with David. Doesn't he look nice and all grown up?" she said, flitting her hands around him without touching.

"Why yes, Amanda, he certainly does," Mrs. Johnson said in a high voice. Emily had come by the screech in her voice naturally. "We'll see if we have time." She smiled pleasantly at Mrs. Blake, but David could see in her small dark eyes that her expression was forced and she lowered her head immediately. Her tiny pointed chin formed a deep V in the folds of her neck. He guessed that down deep she would have liked to tell Mrs. Blake exactly what she thought of her "educated Indian."

David often found Mrs. Blake's domineering attitude embarrassing and exasperating, but at times like this, he was glad to have her on his side. "Nice to see you Mrs. Johnson," he said in a voice smooth as syrup with his nicest smile. "And you too, Mr. Johnson." David had learned that when someone obviously disliked him, the best course was to shower them with friendliness. It gave them no option but to painfully grin and bear it.

Meanwhile, Levi Johnson stared at the Blakes's wagon intently. His smoldering blue eyes burned beneath thick, almost white eyebrows. Frowning without answering, he roughly put his arm around Emily as if to shield her. David heard him mutter under his breath, "You can dress him up all you want, but he's still a goddamned Indian."

He felt Levi Johnson's hatred burn but he held his smile as they passed the house. His stomach felt queasy and he wished his back wasn't exposed to the big man.

Mrs. Blake's neck turned beet red against her tan dress. She neither turned around nor acknowledged Johnson's comment. Her back remained perfectly straight, and her focus remained straight ahead. Amanda Blake was not one to let a man like Levi Johnson spoil her day in the sun.

Just down the road, three women stood in the shade of the weathered gray barn of the livery stable. The building had leaned three or four feet to the left while David was away. The roof was still perfectly parallel with the ground, and the slanting the walls had creating a perfect trapezoid . . . or was it a parallelogram? He had forgotten his geometry so quickly. The livery reminded him of a very large, tired person about to fall asleep on his feet.

Amanda's lean face brightened as they neared the women and she began introducing them to David. The homestead housewives were nearly indistinguishable from one another to David. He didn't remember any of them, but based on the way Mrs. Blake was talking, they all knew his story. In fact, it seemed that everyone knew his story. Keeping up his forced smile, he longed for the anonymity of the city. An Indian dressed like a white person was mostly white in the East, but still mostly Indian in the West.

They were fifty feet from Warner's store now. There was a crowd of men gathered around an empty buckboard wagon in front of the store. Perched on the seat of the wagon was an outlandish figure. Dressed in a fringed buckskin outfit and large floppy hat, waving his arms and gesturing wildly, David recognized Rafe Colton from the train.

"How can a store be closed? We have the biggest hunt in America going on right here in this little armpit of a town and we can't even get provisions?" he shouted. "Newspaperman," he called out at Terrel, who was standing off to the left. "Make these people understand how important this hunt is."

The group turned expectantly toward the reporter, but before he could answer a dark-haired woman in a blue calico dress stepped toward the wagon. David recognized Mrs. Warner.

"As I told you Mr.—ummmm—is it Colman?" she said in a most patient voice. "The store—"

"It's Colton, C-O-L-T-O-N," he blustered as he stood up on the wagon seat, towering over the group. "Rafe Colton, wilderness scout, Indian fighter and—"

"Colton," she interrupted, firmly holding up a piece of paper. "Mr. Colton, as I told you several times, the order you have here would deplete most of our supplies and my husband is not available to make the appropriate arrangements. I expect him back anytime. You'll just have to wait until he returns."

David could see her eyes darting from the wagon to the men standing around it, looking for a friendly face.

"Rafe Colton waits for no man or woman or store," he bellowed. "We will persevere without those stores if need be. Why, back in '89 I spent most of a year living off nothing but grasshoppers and sunflower seeds. The Indians had us pinned down and . . ."

Deloris spotted the Blakes's wagon pulling up to the edge of the group and made her way out of the crowd of men. "Amanda, Edward, thank God you're here," she said.

"Why, Deloris, don't you want to say hello to David?" Amanda replied, patting David on the shoulder. "Doesn't he look all grown up in his nice suit?"

"Hello, Mrs. Warner," David said smiling brightly and holding out his hand.

"Oh yes, hello, David," Deloris said distractedly as she lightly touched David's hand and turned toward Mr. Blake. "Edmund, please help us. James and Evan went out to the Badlands yesterday to hunt that damned sheep. They haven't come back yet." The corners of her eyes were moist and sparkled in the late afternoon light.

"Oh, now, Deloris," he said in his deep slow voice. "I'm sure they're just camping out somewhere so they could get a good early start today." He smoothed his brushy mustache with his fingers. "There's nothing to worry about."

Deloris shook her head. "James hates sleeping outside. I asked Bill Baxter to go out and get Morgan this morning but I haven't heard from either of them," she persisted, with a tinge of panic in her voice. "He didn't know if he would find Morgan." She wiped her cheek with the back of her hand.

Despite her attempt to keep her conversation quiet, some of the strangers were growing tired of Rafe Colton's stories and moved over closer to the Blakes's wagon. Strangers would never gather around a private conversation in the city, David thought, but entertainment options were few in a place like Interior.

Deloris's face brightened and her dark blue eyes came alive as she turned to David. "Of course, David, you'd know where Evan would take his father to hunt that sheep. You two boys used to practically live out in the Badlands. Could you and Edmund look for them?" David noticed that her fingernails were white as she tightly gripped the side of the wagon.

"Oh, I'm sure that David would never remember any of that," Amanda said waving her hand. "Traipsing around the Badlands is not something David does anymore. Besides, he just got a new suit." She smoothed the suit over his shoulder again.

He looked over at Mrs. Blake's hand on his shoulder. "Mrs. Blake is right, Mrs. Warner, it's been two years since I've been out there and the Badlands change each season," David replied. Amanda nodded and patted him on the arm. "But I'd be happy to go out and do whatever I can to help find Evan and Mr. Warner," he continued. He could feel Mrs. Blake's body tense next to him.

Shooting David a sharp look, Amanda turned to Mr. Blake and said, "Edmund, I don't see how we could have time to have you two rushing out to those Badlands like wild Indians."

"Aheeeemm, Madam." An old man leading an emaciated horse stepped forward and raised his hand slowly. "If'n you could see fit to provide me a small stake, Ah'd be happy to rescue your husband and son," he said in a gravelly voice.

Deloris turned to see that several of the men had gathered around the Blakes's wagon. Before she could answer, a short, pudgy cowboy piped up. "Butch, you don't know nothin' about trackin' or the Badlands. What makes you think you'd do anything but get lost?"

"Ah, hell," Butch shot back in a much too loud voice. "With the right stake, I can rescue folks just as well as—"

"Rescue? If there's a rescue to be made it's Rafe Colton that can perform it," he bellowed, now that the group had migrated away from him. "Who's missing? Why, I can track a June beetle through a snowstorm . . . "

Another stranger piped in, "She lost her husband and son. They got lost in the Badlands tracking the sheep."

A tall cowboy whose face was being overtaken by a huge black beard added, "Probably got scalped by those damned ghost Injuns out there."

David felt detached from the comments about the Indians until he caught the eye of one of the cowboys staring directly at him.

"Rafe Colton is not afraid of Injuns, ghostwise or otherwise," the man declared. He ran his hand over the brim of his hat, loudly sniffed several times and pinched his nose. "Now if you can get me an article of clothing from your husband, my good lady, I will track him through the wilds of the Badlands." He looked over at Terrel and winked broadly. "Might make a good story."

Edmund reached across Amanda and David to touch Deloris's fingers on the edge of the wagon. "Deloris," he said kindly, "I think the best course of action is to wait until we find Morgan. A bunch of people rushing out to the Badlands this late in the day won't help anyone."

Deloris looked at the men gathered around her. She took a deep breath and said very quietly, "Edmund, you are probably right." She pulled a stray strand of her dark hair back and stepped away from the Blakes's wagon.

Amanda broke in quickly, "Well, with all that settled we must be going. We have several people who want to see David." She moved her hand to Edmund's arm to take the reins from him.

Edmund held the reins firmly and said reassuringly to Deloris. "David and I will check back in an hour or two, just before dark. If they aren't back by then and if you haven't heard from Morgan, we'll organize a search party to look for them in the morning."

Deloris gave him a relieved smile and turned to the group of men around her. "Mr. Blake has assured me that my husband and son are most likely just fine. Just a mother's worry is all. Thank you all very much for your offers of help," she said in a strong voice. "Our store will be closed until tomorrow." She moved quickly through the crowd to the back door.

The crowd of men started to disperse, most following behind Rafe Colton's wagon as it headed to the tent camp on the outside of town. Edmund clicked his tongue and the Blakes's wagon slowly rattled along in the opposite direction. David could feel the hostility from Mrs. Blake but she said nothing. He smiled to himself at his pride in Mr. Blake. He also looked forward to getting away from the stares of the tall cowboy and his friends.

"I see them! I see them coming in!" a young voice shouted. A small boy ran down the street, dust kicking up with each of his footsteps. Once he saw he had people's attention, he turned and pointed toward the spires of the Badlands.

In the distance, more than a quarter-mile away, three men and a horse came into view. One man was slumped in the saddle. The other two were walking alongside. In the late afternoon light, small heat waves rippled the through the images, blending and unblending them with the backdrop of the Badlands.

The boy, Jimmie Baxter, ran to the back door of Warner's Store and pounded on it. "Mrs. Warner, Mrs. Warner, I see them. They're back!"

The door opened quickly and Deloris stepped out with a wooden spoon in her hand. She dropped it into the dust as Jimmie grabbed her hand with both of his and pulled her to the road. "Thank God!" she whispered and strode briskly out toward them.

Jimmie ran back down the street toward the three figures slowly making their way into town. With a sense of exhilaration, David started to get up from the wagon to run with him but Amanda put a hand on his arm. He sat back down with the other adults. He wished he could run with the kids again.

With a "Heeeahhhh" and the rattle of wagon wheels, rapid hoofbeats and the snap of a whip, Rafe Colton's wagon thundered down the road at full gallop toward the three figures. They were barely visible through the dust kicked up by the wagon.

Shading his eyes with his hand, David watched the wagon make a wild turn, bouncing as it pulled up next to the figures in the distance. The man on the horse was pulled off and helped onto the seat of the wagon next to Colton. David recognized the man climbing up on the horse replacing the injured man. Nobody sat a horse like Morgan.

Colton's wagon made its way back to town only slightly slower than when it left, and Jimmie ran back down the street, crying out, "Mr. Warner's hurt."

"He get shot?" the pudgy cowboy standing in front of Warner's store asked.

"Who got shot? Are the damn Indians shooting?" the tall black-bearded man shouted.

The wagon thundered up in front of the store and stopped with a lurch. James Warner sat next to Colton, with his injured leg elevated on the footrest, still splinted with the old rifle. He looked around him, taking in the crowd in front of the store.

"Who shot you, James?" a male voice called out. He looked up in surprise.

"Ain't nobody shot nobody!" a harsh voice growled from the dust cloud behind the wagon. "We don't need no goddamned rumors," Morgan said in disgust as he reined in Blue. "James got his knee twisted and Evan here got him out." He pointed to the back of the wagon where the boy sat facing back toward the Badlands, his feet dangling out the back.

Evan slid off the wagon to face the crowd. He had grown four or five inches taller than David remembered and was thin as a rail. His face was caked with dirt. He gave Morgan a crooked smile.

"Yes," James spoke up from the seat of the wagon. "We got ourselves into a tight spot and had to spend the night out there. Just me and the boy." He glanced back at Evan and nodded. "It hurts like the dickens. It's a good thing Morgan found us this morning or I'd'a had to crawl out."

"You look like you could use a drink, Warner," Levi Johnson called out. "You got any of that rotgut left?"

"Yessir, Mr. Warner," Rafe Colton said as he clapped him on the back. "Now that I got you rescued, let's talk some business. I need supplies for our hunt and I got an Englishman's cash to spend. Heh, heh, heh."

"Come on in, then," James said, waving his hand. "Deloris, we gotta get the store open for these boys!"

The men cheered and two of them helped James down from the wagon. Deloris walked quickly back to where Evan was standing. She slipped her arms around him and rested her head on his thin shoulder. "Mom, you're going to get all dirty," he said, his lips barely moving. He waved his arms for an instant before awkwardly putting them around his mother's back.

"I'm so glad you're home," she said, hugging him harder and pulling his face to her shoulder. Evan buried his face deeply into his mother's shoulder looking for an instant more like a five-year-old than almost a man.

David slid down from the wagon, ignoring Amanda's hand closing on his arm. Morgan leaned over from his horse toward Mrs. Warner as she stood hugging her son. "Deloris, he did real good out there. Better than 'most any man," he drawled.

Through the tears in her eyes Deloris said, "Thank you Morgan. Won't you come in for some dinner?" She reached up to put a hand on his arm. The half-smile froze on his face as he focused on the pale hand resting on the sleeve of his worn blue shirt. He nodded.

"Deloris," James yelled from inside the store. "Where's the rest of the whiskey?"

She smiled and slid her hand off Morgan's arm. He immediately busied himself pulling out his watch and studied it intently. "See you after you've washed up then," she said as she gave Evan a last squeeze, waved to Edmund and Amanda and walked into the store, the skirt of her blue dress swinging.

"Evan, that was really quite amazing!" David said with a smile, holding out his hand. Evan's eyes were still watery and red. There were a few muddy tracks of tears flowing from the corners of his eyes. He forgot to hide them as his face lit up at the sight of his longtime pal.

Evan's face had elongated and his beak nose dominated his face. David thought he looked like an older brother to the boy he had once known.

"Gosh, David it's good to see you," he said looking down at David's extended hand. The boys had never shaken hands before, but he awkwardly gripped the hand and shook it gently. David unconsciously wiped off the dirt on the back of his pants. They looked at each other awkwardly, searching for a place to put their hands.

"And, Morgan. How long has it been?" he asked moving toward the man on his horse and holding out his hand.

The old rancher slowly pulled off one dirty leather glove and leaned down to grip David's hand firmly. "It's been an age, that is for sure," Morgan answered.

"How did you ever get him out of the Badlands on horseback with that leg?" David asked, looking up at Morgan.

Evan swiftly responded, waving his hands, eager to tell the story himself. "We used a travois and had Blue pull it," he said, the words tumbling out in a flourish. "Pa made us take it apart once we got out of the Badlands. He said he wasn't going to go back to town like a god-damned Indian's papoose." He laughed a little too loudly and looked at Morgan for approval. Evan's deepening voice with the occasional crack sounded to David like it should be coming from a different person than the one he knew. But the enthusiastic flow of words definitely came from the Evan he remembered.

The old rancher smiled, showing dark yellowed teeth. "Evan here was the hero. He knows it, I know it and James knows it. I'm right proud of him," he said, winking at Evan.

The thin boy beamed. "Aw Morgan, if you wouldn't'a showed up, we would'a had to . . ." his voice trailed off.

"Evan," James's voice came from the inside of the store. "I thought I told you to take out the garbage before we left. Git in here and take it out."

Evan's smile faded. He looked at Morgan and then David. "Guess I'm needed inside. You comin' in?" he asked.

"Ah'll take care of Blue and wash up a little. Then I'll be in." Morgan said as he dismounted. He seemed considerably older and shorter than David remembered.

David looked over to the Blake's wagon. "I'll stop in later, Evan, and we can get reacquainted. I think Mrs. Blake has some additional stops for me to make." He formally reached out to shake hands with both Evan and Morgan in the manner prescribed by the Pierceson School. They both looked a little more at ease with the hand-shaking routine this time. He walked to the Blakes's wagon and leapt up, wondering if the jump would rip the pants of his new suit.

"Glad you're all right, Evan," Mr. Blake shouted as he flipped the reins. David waved and Mrs. Blake stared straight ahead, her back extremely straight.

Chapter Eight

IT WAS ANOTHER TWO HOURS before David made it back to the store. Mrs. Blake insisted that they visit every one of the little homesteads in the valley so David could "say hello." He noticed the frozen smiles on the women as they deftly shook his hand and remarked about how grown up he was. He could feel the undercurrent of fear. He wondered if they would have been more comfortable if he'd shown up in war paint.

However, Mrs. Blake must have been satisfied. She only protested mildly when he said he wanted to stop by Warner's store and that he'd walk home. Edmund supported him, "Now Amanda, he's visited all your friends, let him visit his friends." He gently pushed David off the wagon seat. "Be home for dinner in an hour or so."

"Yessir." He slid off the wagon and quickly walked toward the store before Mrs. Blake could change her mind.

The shabby little store hadn't changed in the two years he'd been away. The door still squeaked as he pulled it open and he was immediately hit with the smells of kerosene, tobacco, dust and sweat.

There was still a crowd of men inside. Rafe Colton leaned against the back counter, flanked by two of the cowboys who had been standing beside his wagon earlier. Terrel, the newspaperman, stood next to them with a drink in his hand. James Warner was sitting behind the counter with his injured leg propped up. From the several empty bottles on the counter, it appeared that Colton had been buying rounds.

"You otter be writin' this down, noosepaberman," Colton slurred as he slapped Terrel on the back. "It isn't every day you get an heckclusive interview with a wild west legend."

Terrel caught David's eye and smiled. "I got it all right here, Rafe," he said, pointing to his temple. "Your stories tend to stick with a man a long time. A long, long time."

"An' don't forget to get the story of my buddy James here." Colton pointed at Evan's father. "Surviving alone in the Badlands with a broke leg while huntin' that big sheep should make a goooood story."

"Come on, Rafe," a short, pudgy cowboy said. "Pour another round and tell us more about Indian fightin'."

Colton didn't need much encouragement. "Yeah, get my buddy Bob the packhorse-man another drink," he said as he slapped the little man on the back. As he eagerly held out his jar, it was pretty clear Bob was more interested in the drink than the story. The other cowboy, a large athletic man with a black beard hiding his face, put his glass forward as well. "An' one for ol' Drager too, that mean son of a bitch." Colton shakily poured a drink for each of the men and took a drink himself, straight from the bottle. "It was back in '88, I think. I was scoutin' for General Perry on the Costa Mesa . . ."

In the opposite corner of the store, Morgan sat at the little checker table leaning back on his chair, with his hat pulled low. His eyes were nearly closed and his worn boots barely touched the floor. Evan sat beside him, listening to Colton's Indian tales and glowering. It was evident from the look on his face that he was doing a slow burn.

Evan leaned over to Morgan and said in a voice that David heard from the front of the store, "I bet that sumbitch never even saw an Indian that wasn't standin' in front of some big city drug store." Morgan grunted but his face didn't move and his eyes didn't open.

"Evan, Morgan, good evening," David said as he walked toward the little table in the corner.

Evan jumped up, bumping the table and sloshing Morgan's drink. "Great to see you, David." He awkwardly held out his hand and David shook it.

Morgan cursed under his breath at the half-spilled drink and nonchalantly tipped his hat.

"Ummm . . . sorry, Morgan," Evan said as he noticed the whiskey on the table and tried to wipe it off with his hand.

The old rancher barely moved his lips. "Beyond me, how the man that could figure out how to climb down that chute could be the clumsiest oaf in the country," he grumbled with just a hint of a smile.

In the light of the kerosene lamp, the lines in Morgan's face looked deeper than ever.

Evan beamed at being called a man as he sat back down, and David felt a twinge of envy. "So, Evan, tell me about your great adventure hunting this mountain sheep," he said, pulling a chair up to the little table.

"Awww, Pa wanted me to take him to the ram so he could shoot him," Evan replied. Then, leaning close to David and dropping his voice to a whisper, he said, "I didn't take 'im nowhere close to where I saw him. I'm saving him for us."

David's eyes widened. "Us? What do you mean *us*?" He put his arms on the table to steady it before Evan spilled Morgan's drink again.

Before Evan could answer, Terrel moved across the room, leaned against a nearby post and spoke over David's shoulder. "Does it bother you hearing the great Indian fighter Colton and that Drager guy rant on and on about the evil redskins?"

David was a little surprised at the question. He hadn't considered being offended. The unstated but understood mission at the Pierceson School was "Kill the Indian, save the man." He had stopped thinking of himself as a person who'd be offended by insults to Indians a long time ago. For him, evil redskins were characters in dime novels, just the same as they were to other educated people.

Before he could answer, Evan piped in, "That bastard's been shootin' his mouth off all night about bein' an Indian fighter. Morgan here's twice the fighter that bastard will ever be. He was at Wounded Knee!"

Morgan's eyes snapped open and he brought his chair to the floor with a thud. He glared fiercely at Evan, who shrank back in his seat and tried to make himself smaller.

"Really, Mr. Morgan," Terrel said, reaching inside his coat for his writing pad and focusing his attention on the old rancher. "You were at Wounded Knee?"

Still glaring at Evan, Morgan asserted in a quiet, rough voice, "No, not me. Boy here's mistaken."

Terrel was undeterred. "I did a story last year about a group that wants to take the Medals of Honor away from the men who fought in that battle. It seems Indian fighting doesn't have the same glamour now that we are in the new century. What do you think? Should we still honor Indian fighters?"

Morgan looked directly at Terrel for the first time. His thick eyebrows couldn't hide the intensity in his cold blue eyes. "Killin' ain't fightin'," he said very quietly.

An uneasy silence loomed as the reporter stood frozen with his mouth and notepad open. Morgan released him from his stare and finished his drink in one gulp. He slowly rose and ambled toward the door with a slight limp.

"Sorry, Morgan," Evan said meekly to his back. He paused for a second, but proceeded out the front door without looking back.

David watched Evan's face fall.

Terrel regained his composure. "He was obviously lying. What can you tell me about it?" he asked, turning aggressively to Evan.

Before he could answer, David replied, "You heard Morgan. He said he wasn't there. Isn't a man's word good enough for you? " He rose from his chair and stood directly between Evan and Terrel.

Without hesitation, the reporter promptly switched his focus to David. "As an Indian, what do you think about taking the Medals of Honor away from the soldiers at Wounded Knee?" he asked, tapping his pencil on his pad.

"As an Indian," David said slowly, looking directly into Terrel's eyes and carefully enunciating each syllable. "I want no part of your bullshit." He gave Terrel his sweetest and broadest smile, then turned away and sat back down with Evan.

The young reporter showed his teeth briefly and clucked his tongue at the rebuke. "Guess I'll go back to some more quotable sources," he said, nodding across the room. "There is no lack of quotes over there." He gave them a slight wave as he turned away and walked slowly over to where Colton was pouring another round.

"That guy's a nuisance," David said to Terrel's retreating back.

"God, Morgan looked mad," Evan sighed, looking toward the front door. "I didn't mean to say anything. It was just that I was so sick of listening to them shoot their mouths off." He nodded over to where

Colton and James were now sitting together. As he had countless times already, James was demonstrating how he'd moved his hands to climb down the crack with his injured knee.

"Was Morgan really at Wounded Knee?" David asked, looking seriously into Evan's eyes.

Evan nodded. "Yeah, he told me. He was in the army. He didn't say anything about what he did there, but he said he used one of those big hotchscotch guns."

"Hotchkiss," David said with a smile. "I did a paper on weaponry at school. They fired over thirty rounds per minute."

"Yeah, Hotchkiss is right," Evan nodded his head quickly. He paused for a second and leaned toward David. "He said your pa was there too."

David furrowed his brow. "Mr. Blake? I never heard . . ."

"No," Evan said in a whisper, "your real pa. Morgan said his name was Stone Eagle." He pointed over his shoulder at the wanted poster.

David studied the poster and then turned back to Evan. "The Blakes are my family."

"But Morgan said . . ." Evan stammered, nervously jostling the table.

"I told you. I don't have any other family," David said coldly, his expression indicating that the subject was closed.

Evan sighed deeply. The elation he had felt earlier was completely gone. He now looked like a miserable little kid. David knew he meant well, but he was treading on territory they had never visited before and he didn't want to start now. His friend had always had a nasty habit of blurting out whatever was on his mind and it appeared he hadn't learned much discretion over the last two years. David's heritage was a matter he would not discuss.

"So tell me about this sheep in the Badlands," he said to break the silence and put his friend at ease.

Evan's face lit up again, hoping the change of subject would help them forget the earlier conversation. "David, you should have seen it. I was scouting out on Mystic Mountain for when we go to hunt and I could see him standin' up at the top of the bowl, just looking at me," Evan said, words tumbling out him. "All the times we was out in the Badlands and we never saw him. An' then just like that, I see him!" Evan was sitting on the edge of his seat, gripping the table so hard with both hands that it shook.

David smiled. The look in Evan's eyes was the same one he had seen countless times when they were kids. He would get so excited about things that he couldn't sit still. He was like an eight year-old kid trying to escape an almost-grown body.

"So who do you think will finally kill it? I know you and your father went out. With him hurt will you hunt alone or with Morgan?"

"Ahhhh, poof! My Pa just wanted to shoot him so he could put the head up in the store to bring in customers. I never took him even close to where the ram really was." Evan smiled broadly, savoring the moment. "I saved him for you an' me. It'll be like old times. We can track him down out in the Badlands just like we used to hunt. An' we'll be famous."

"Me?" David said with astonishment, bringing his hands to his chest. "Why would I want to traipse around in the Badlands after a sheep? We have several people to see and I have a paper to write before school again."

Evan's face fell yet again. While David had no intention of sounding so harsh, his answer had caught Evan completely off guard. He couldn't grasp that, for David, the very thought of going from successful student to some sort of ragtag hunter was ludicrous. For two years they had been removing the Indian part of him. It didn't make sense to run around the Badlands now.

"Evan, I'm sorry to disappoint you," he said in a conciliatory tone. "Hunting just doesn't hold my interest anymore."

Evan gripped the table hard. "What do you mean don't hold your interest? You telling me you want to sit around in your fancy clothes, drinkin' tea with old ladies and readin' books instead'a huntin' in the Badlands? Who are you anyway?"

David felt the blood rush to his head and he was a little dizzy. "I'm not an eight-year-old hick kid is what I'm not," he snapped. "If you want to waste your time scrambling around out in that hell hole, go right ahead. I'm not like that anymore. The real hunters are the ones who'll kill him anyway." He nodded over to where Colton was continuing to hold court. He knew this was a low blow to Evan and immediately regretted saying it.

Evan narrowed his eyes and stared across the store. He turned back to David. "The kid I used to play with was more of a man than you'll ever be," he said through clenched teeth. He shoved back the table and stalked toward the front door.

"Evan! Evan, where are you goin'?" James called from the other end of the store. "We need 'nother bottle."

"Get it yourself!" Evan snapped at his father. "I need some air. Too damn many mature adults in here for me." He looked back at David as he went out the door, slamming it shut behind him.

David couldn't believe it. He hadn't talked to Evan in more than two years and in their first ten minutes together they had their first-ever fight. What had happened to his friend? Why did he, like everybody else, want him to be someone else?

"Your friends all seem to be upset tonight," Terrel said with a smug smile, as he walked back across the room with another drink in his hand.

"You certainly didn't help any," David retorted without turning to look at him. He had liked the reporter when they met on the train, but his questioning of Morgan and Evan wasn't right.

"Oh, you just don't understand journalism." Terrel slid into Evan's chair with a self-satisfied grin. "I get paid to ask the hard questions. You don't always make friends."

David thought about arguing with him, but decided that he had created enough enemies for the night. "I can't figure it out. It's like he's eight years old or something."

"You mean your young friend Evan? From what I've gathered," he said with a nod toward Colton, James and company, "he probably saved his father's life yesterday out in the Badlands. Not that his old man would admit it."

David was surprised. He thought Morgan had been patronizing Evan to make him feel important. "Evan, you mean? I mean that's great and all, but I have a hard time picturing Evan Warner as a great wilderness hero."

The reporter swirled the liquor in his jar and gave David a knowing look. "It seems everyone has a hard time not thinking of him as a little kid."

David let his eyes flick up to the ceiling. "It seems like everything has changed," he said partly to himself. "And I'm not exactly sure who I'm supposed to be."

Terrel stood up. "Well, Rafe Colton, Indian fighter, wilderness scout, et cetera et cetera, always knows what role he's playing. However obnoxious that it is," he added. He smiled broadly. "I better get back or they won't let me be their exclusive reporter." He rose and sauntered back over to the counter.

David looked around the store. The place had seemed so familiar, almost like home, two years ago and even when he arrived this evening. Now he felt like a stranger. He stood and quietly walked to the door without saying goodbye to anyone.

Chapter Nine

THE FRESH, COOL NIGHT AIR was a welcome relief and it cleared David's head. The planks of the little boardwalk squeaked as he sprang onto the hard-packed road. *Great,* he thought. *Back home for one day and I've already made people mad.*

The laughter and voices from the store faded as he strode down the middle of the road toward the Blakes's house on the outskirts of town. He hated having people mad at him. Everything was just so different. Even the quiet of the prairie evening, as it crept over the town, almost hurt his ears. It had been a long time since he'd noticed the crunch of his own feet on an unpaved road.

Back at school, everything was clear. He had to stop being an Indian, everyone told him so. It was the 1900s. Men did not run around in loincloths. They dressed properly and got an education so they would be respected.

But he didn't feel respected. Now that he was back in Dakota, he found that people didn't respect education, especially in an Indian. They feared it. He was just another Indian, and once a savage always a savage.

There were certainly no streetlights in Interior. Looking up, he noticed the stars for the first time in months. Even when he could see the stars in the city, he never took the time to look. The little sliver of a moon cast faint shadows around the abandoned buildings at this end of the street. Random junk discarded between the structures became unrecognizable dark shapes within the shadows.

He cut the corner by the livery stable to save a few steps and get to the warm light of the Blakess' house as soon as possible. Out of the darkness beside the building a hulking figure stepped in front of him. Startled, he instinctively glanced over his shoulder toward the store and the last bit of manmade light in town to see if there was anyone he could look to for help if he needed it, but the street was empty.

"Excuse me," he said with far more bravado than he felt. "Is something the matter?"

In the dim light he could only see the profile of the man. He had long hair like an Indian and was big and wide, taller than David but hulking. His body odor was overwhelming. Once in front of him, the big man didn't move and made no sound. He just loomed in front of David.

David was no coward. But the man had just appeared out of nowhere and there was nobody to help him. He hadn't felt so alone, so detached, in a long time.

"I've got to get home," he took a step to the side and kept up his false bravado as he moved to get around the big man. Then he felt a hand on his chest gently pushing him back.

"Crow Eyes," the man croaked in a deep voice. "You are Crow Eyes."

David backed away, away from the hand, settling into a defensive crouch. "You're mistaken. My name is David Blake. You must be looking for somebody else. I've got to get home," he said.

"You are Crow Eyes and I'm Stone Eagle," the big man said. "Your father."

David felt a burning starting in his stomach and rising to his throat. He found himself trying to look the big man in the eyes, but couldn't see them. "I don't know who or what you are, but you don't have anything to do with me."

"I had to let you go," the dark figure said. "Let me explain."

David looked at the shadowy figure. With every fiber in his body he wanted to avoid the man, the words, the situation. Electric currents ran through his body, pushing blood to his muscles.

"I have to go now," David said firmly, raising his hands in front of him instinctively. He took a breath, then said, "They are looking for you, you know. You should go someplace else." He wished he had never heard of this man.

Stone Eagle mumbled. "There is no other place."

"I don't care where you go or what you do," David said forcefully as he moved around the man. "Just leave me alone!"

With surprising speed, Stone Eagle grabbed David by the lapels of his suit and said, "Please, let me ex—"

Instinctively, David shot a left jab straight into the big man's face, just as the boxing coach had taught them at school. He felt a satisfying splat against his knuckles. The hands lost their grip on his suit as David pivoted and finished the job by ripping a savage right cross to the big man's face.

Stone Eagle collapsed into the dirt.

David felt the adrenaline surging through his body. He shook his bruised right hand and backed away from where Stone Eagle lay crumpled on the road. "Just leave here, and don't ever talk to me again," he commanded, his voice shaking with emotion. "You don't have anything to do with me."

He turned and strode away, never looking back. He had never hit anyone outside of boxing club practice. The bare knuckle blows hurt his hands. His legs seemed to have a mind of their own as they carried him from the livery stable to the welcome light of the Blakes's house. As his heart rate slowed, though, he wondered, *is the man really Stone Eagle, and is he really my father?*

The familiar glow in the front window seemed to warm his body. Between the ruffled curtains, he saw Mrs. Blake walking into the sitting room with a tray of tea. He started to jog to the door, toward the warmth of lamplight and a rocking chair in front of a warm fire with a cup of tea in his hand. Jogging away from . . . whatever that was on the street behind him.

The one thing that he did know for sure was that the hulking, stinking figure lying in the dirt by the livery stable couldn't possibly be any part of him. Not now, not ever.

Chapter Ten

STONE EAGLE LAY MOTIONLESS in the dirt by the livery stable. The blow from Crow Eyes hurt him more than he could ever admit.

"You can't expect him to understand," a quiet voice said from the shadows.

He rolled over and looked toward the sound. He'd forgotten Fire Brush was standing behind the building. He didn't want to hear from him now and only grunted in response.

"Stone Eagle, don't stay here . . . here in this town. He's right. We need to go."

The big man shook his head and spit some blood into the dirt. "Leave me alone. Go back to wherever you came from."

Fire Brush let out a little laugh and reached over to help him up. "Everyone leaves you alone, Stone Eagle."

He groaned as he got to his feet. "What are you doing here, anyway? I didn't ask you to follow me."

"I don't have anywhere to go, either." He took the big man's arm and led him toward the rear of the building. "You wanted to tell him why you left him here. Tell me. Maybe that will help. You need to tell someone."

They sat against the back wall. Stone Eagle was still breathing hard and his head hurt. He didn't understand why this man wouldn't leave him alone. He didn't understand why his son wouldn't listen to him. He didn't understand anything anymore.

He leaned his head back against the rough wood of the building and looked up at the stars in the fall sky. He'd carried the story inside him for a long time. During those nights in the Black Hills he'd always thought he might be able to tell it to his son one day. He would understand. He would forgive.

Almost without thinking, he started talking in a low, hoarse voice.

"I was never a warrior or hunter. I learned to hunt, of course, like all the other boys. And I fought—sometimes winning, sometimes losing—but I never enjoyed it like the others. As I hunted and fought less and less, they laughed at me more and more. The 'warriors' . . . they were only boys playing games from times lost. We had no war. We had no great hunts. Our food came from the *Wasichus*. We had no one to fight but each other. But still, they played and hunted like somehow it would make a difference." Stone Eagle shook his head.

Fire Brush's quiet reply startled him: "At least you got a chance to hunt, to be Lakota. You're lucky. You don't know what it's like in those schools.

"I don't know schools," Stone Eagle said. "I just know it isn't like the old stories. Warriors living a past they don't even understand."

Taking a deep breath, he continued. "I tended the horses for our tribe and the soldiers. Animals, they listen to me." He paused and wiped the sweat from his brow. He stared at the ground in front of him, lost in the images in his mind. "They listened to me then. I was paid gold and I bought horses. I gave Blunt Knife ten horses and he gave me his daughter Spring Bird to be my wife." Stone Eagle ran his hand over the ground, smoothing the dirt between his legs. "No warrior could get ten horses to give for a wife. We couldn't leave the reservation. Where could a warrior get horses?

"But she wanted a warrior husband. She laughed at me and called me a coward, but she was happy to live in my lodge and eat my food. Could a warrior have given her that? Could he?"

Fire Brush shook his head but said nothing.

"But she gave me a son. Crow Eyes, we called him until he earned a name of his own, because his eyes were always alive and dancing like the eyes of a crow. He was a beautiful baby. I lived for him. I would rather spend time with him than work or play or hunt or . . . or be with Spring Bird."

He took a deep breath, his big chest heaving. "When Sitting Bull was killed, I wanted to stay at Standing Rock, but Spring Bird wanted to go with the band to the south. She said the soldiers would come and they would take Crow Eyes. They would kill all the Lakota children."

"And so we ran. We ran from our warm lodge and horses and gold. We ran to the cold, to the south, to the Badlands, to *O-ona-gazhee*, the Stronghold, to the Ghost Dance. The warrior boys got their way. They thought they were Crazy Horse or Sitting Bull or Red Cloud, but they weren't. They were just boys with guns and dreams in the cold plains north of the Badlands." Stone Eagle shook his head and spit into the dirt, the taste of blood still in his mouth.

"When they caught us at Wounded Knee creek, it was over. We all knew it was over. There would be no war. There would be no Ghost Dance. There would be no return to the old ways. What use did I have for the old ways? I only wanted to go back to my warm lodge with my son and tend horses.

"That cold morning, we all stood together around Big Foot. He was so sick he could barely stand. The warriors gathered close to him, the women and children around the edges. All three hundred of us stood there cold and hungry. Spring Bird held our son close to her chest to keep him warm. I stood beside her to warm his other side. She turned to me and said, 'Why aren't you standing with Big Foot with your gun? Why aren't you with my brothers and the other warriors? Why aren't you protecting your people?' I looked around at the warriors gathered close to Big Foot. The young ones were shouting at the soldiers.

"Big Foot told them to put their weapons in a pile like the soldiers said but they were shouting back. The young warriors wanted to fight. They had never been in a war. I had thrown away my old rifle, days ago. It was too cold—too heavy and I didn't like to shoot. I was the only man not standing with Big Foot in the front."

"Spring Bird's eyes blazed at me. 'Go, go and fight!' she said. Her words cut through the cold air like a knife to my heart. She put her hands on my chest and pushed me. Pushed me away from my son!" Stone Eagle paused, his breath rattling in his throat.

"Then the sound of a shot filled the valley," he continued. "Everything was silent for a moment. Then the warriors raised their weapons and the women and children ran down the ravine for cover." Stone Eagle paused again and licked his dry cracked lips. "All the men but me," he said. "I ran to protect my son. I ran away to protect my son." He clenched his fist in front of him.

"Then there was gunfire from everywhere. The smoke from the guns filled the whole ravine. We ran. Spring Bird with Crow Eyes and the other women ran down the valley, tripping over each other in the snow. They clawed at one another to get free—free of the guns and smoke and noise. And I ran with them. When the smoke cleared for an instant, I saw bodies falling. Soldiers were on the sides of the ravine pouring down gunfire.

"The ravine bent around a corner and we ran to where there wasn't any smoke. As we turned the corner we faced a big cannon gun. It could fire again and again pouring bullets at us. There was no sound but the guns. There was no smell but gunpowder. I saw Spring Bird fall and jumped on her to cover our son. The bullets rained down on us.

"And then there was silence." He paused, breathing heavily into the night air.

"The smoke slowly lifted and I looked around at the pile of bodies in the snow. I raised my head and I was looking into Spring Bird's dead face. There was a trickle of blood running out of her mouth. Our son was squirming below me. I opened her dress and pulled him out to hold him close. He was alive and unhurt.

"I stood. The bullets had not found me. Me or my son. I looked at the bodies. I couldn't move my feet. There must have been thirty women and children in that little ravine, and one horse tender and his son. We were the only ones alive.

"I looked up at the big gun. The barrel was still smoking. Soldiers were standing watching me. I heard one of the soldiers say, 'Look at that. Ran away with the women and didn't get shot!' My son was crying so I stepped over the dead bodies of my wife and the other women and children and walked back up the ravine to what was left of the camp."

The two men sat still in the soundless night. Stone Eagle looked over at Fire Brush's dark form, his dark eyes flashing in the starlight. "Why didn't the bullets find me? Why didn't I die with my wife and her sister and the other Lakota? Why did I have to live on?" A single tear tracked down the cheek of his dusty, prematurely aged face.

"You did what you needed to do to save your son," Fire Brush said matter-of-factly without looking up.

"Spring Bird's father never understood that. He lost two of his daughters and all of his sons that day, but he blamed me." Stone Eagle paused again. "He said I should have died running for our weapons like a warrior."

"After that day, the dreams started. Every night I would dream of the cold and smoke and the sounds of shots ringing in my head. And then the smoke would clear and I would stand holding my son in a sea of bodies. All dead, all bloody. Spring Bird, her sisters, many people who weren't even there. And the soldiers on the hill were laughing. Laughing at me. And then the dead bodies were laughing, Spring Bird, too, her white teeth stained with blood as she laughed at me. And I looked my son and he laughed at me too." Stone Eagle's body was shaking. "And then visions of that day came to me when I was not asleep, the smoke, the bodies, the sound of the guns. And the laughing. The laughing would fill my brain. Rage would fill my body.

"I was afraid to sleep and I was afraid to be awake." Stone Eagle sobbed softly, his big shoulders heaving. "Every time I saw my son's face I would be reminded of those shots and those bodies and the smoke. And I would go into a rage and I couldn't control what I did. They wanted a warrior, I became a warrior. No one would laugh at me ever again. But there was no war to wage. There was no enemy to fight. So I fought everyone and everything.

"Finally, I knew it was the end," Stone Eagle said calmly, articulating each word. "I couldn't leave my son with the Lakota. I couldn't have him thinking his father was a coward. I couldn't have him growing up a poor Indian with nothing but dreams of days past. My son was not to be a frightened horse tender or a stupid warrior." He clenched a large fist in front of him.

"I took him to the agent man over there." He pointed at the Blakes's house. "I left him with the *Wasichus* so he would never know his father was a coward. He would never be a stupid warrior looking for stupid fights.

"I left. I left for the center of the Black Hills where Indians don't go because of the bad dead spirits. I went to live with the bad dead spirits because they were better than the dead live spirits of my people. There were no reminders of Wounded Knee. I still had the dreams but I was alone and could hurt no one.

"Now I can't stay there either, and the Great Spirit in Bear Butte abandoned me too."

He looked up. "And my son doesn't want to understand."

A drop of blood fell from his mouth and landed in the dust.

"But he has to."

THE TERROR OF STONE EAGLE'S dreams was worse than ever that night, and they haunted him most of the next day. He and Fire Brush had retreated to the dry wash just outside of town where they fell into the soft sand beneath a cottonwood to rest. Stone Eagle thrashed himself awake against the tree, gashing his forehead on the rough bark. He sat up and watched the morning rays of sunlight reflect on the tall clouds above them.

"You are torturing yourself for nothing," Fire Brush said from across the little wash. "That boy isn't part of you anymore. He's not part of any Lakota."

"You don't know anything about my son."

"I know enough. I've been there. He isn't your son anymore. He isn't Lakota anymore. He isn't anything other than what the whites tell him to be."

In the still air of the morning, the silence hung.

"They'll be looking for you. We need to clear out of here."

"I want to try to see my son again."

"Why? So he'll kill you?" Fire Brush spit into the dust. "Stone Eagle, look at yourself."

He looked at the blood on the front of his coat and put a hand to his swollen jaw. He worked it back and forth. "If Crow Eyes learns what happened . . . why it happened . . . maybe the dreams will stop."

He dropped his hand and raised his head. "Something has to stop the dreams. They're worse here, in the Badlands. I can't bear another night of them."

Fire Brush shook his head. "There's nothing but trouble here."

"There isn't anything but trouble."

They rested until midmorning, until thirst and hunger drove them out of the cover of the draw. They returned to the outskirts of town.

Stone Eagle pointed to a large white board house. "That's the agent's house. That's where Crow Eyes is."

"It makes no sense to do this. I—"

Stone Eagle turned to Fire Brush with a wild look in his eyes. "There's nothing left to do."

He rose and made his way to the house with grim determination. He opened the gate in the picket fence and walked to the steps. Glancing over his shoulder, he saw Fire Brush standing on the other side of the fence with his arms crossed.

For a moment, he stood motionless in front of the door on the big porch of the white house. Then he raised his hand and knocked loudly on the door.

There was singing inside the house. A woman's singing. Amanda Blake opened the door and let out a short scream. "Oh my Lord," she gasped, putting her hands to her thin face, her eyes wide with fear.

Stone Eagle struggled to keep his composure and said in a halting voice, "G-g-gone long time. Crow Eyes . . . Should have . . ."

Amanda Blake recognized the intruder. She pulled her shoulders back and stood defiantly with her hands balled up in fists at her hips. "I don't care how long you were gone. We paid you and he is ours now and forever," she said. Her words flowed in a cascading torrent. "You . . . you get out of here and never come back!" She stepped back and lifted her arm. Stone Eagle flinched, thinking she was going to strike him. Instead, she grabbed the edge of the door and slammed it in his face with fury. He could hear some sort of mechanical noise from inside the house.

He stared at the white paint of the closed door without moving. His mind filled with images of the woman holding the baby he had left there so many years ago. He felt his heart thumping against the little bag inside his shirt on his chest. Tears welled in his eyes. A sick acidic taste filled his mouth.

He turned and stumbled through the gate past Fire Brush. His ears were filled with a ringing sound. He slowed to a shuffle, his feet kicking up dust in the road. He floated through a fog. His son was close but far away. The white woman wouldn't talk to him. There had to be a way to take things back, to make Crow Eyes understand. Wild images danced around the edges of his vision. It was hard to see what was real and what wasn't.

"She wouldn't even talk to you!" Fire Brush said. "I told you that we should go. I told you . . . Stone Eagle, are you all right?" He put a hand on the big man's elbow to steady him as he stood swaying.

Stone Eagle's head was pounding and the road seemed to tilt one way and then another. The world around him grew dimmer, as if he were sinking into a cave. He sank deeper and deeper as the darkness overwhelmed him.

Suddenly, his view brightened and a child appeared in the road ahead of him. It was an Indian toddler who looked up at him with wide, dark, frightened eyes. Stone Eagle extended his arms, but as his fingers curled to scoop up the child and hold him to his chest, the image vanished in a cloud of smoke. He waved his empty arms through the smoke searching for the small boy. Smoke filled his eyes and nose and mouth. He searched for the dark, frightened eyes. His ears rang with noise. It sounded like a hundred guns going off at once.

He coughed violently and the smoke instantly cleared. There was no child, no smoke, no guns, only the heat and the dust.

"What is it?" Fire Brush asked, turning Stone Eagle toward him and holding his shaking hands.

Stone Eagle's head hurt and his stomach felt like it was on fire. He closed his eyes to keep the ground from spinning and to keep from seeing any more visions. He staggered to the side of the road and fell to his knees. Fire Brush patted him on the back and held his hair out of the vomit. Stone Eagle groaned. He was afraid to raise his head and open his eyes but allowed Fire Brush to hold him up.

They staggered back to the little wash, Fire Brush laborioiusly supporting Stone Eagle. They collapsed back underneath the tree.

Stone Eagle held his head between his hands. "I thought it would get better, but it only gets worse! Worse and worse." He curled into a ball and slipped into the cave behind his eyes. He didn't ever want to return. From the dark cave he could sense Fire Brush and the outside world, but shut it out. He reached for the leather pouch on his chest, but his hands were shaking too much to pull it out from beneath his shirt. He clutched it through the cloth and lost consciousness in the dust beneath the cottonwood tree.

Chapter Eleven

THE STENCH OF EMPTY BOTTLES and rotting food made Evan want to throw up. It was either that or his father's nagging.

Ever since they'd come back from the Badlands, James had taken every opportunity to order Evan to do stupid chores. Take out the garbage, sweep the floor, restock the shelves, all while he sat on his fat butt, resting his knee and telling stories. In the four days since they got back, James's role in the adventure had increased each day and Evan's had diminished.

"Now it's like I was never even there," he angrily muttered to himself as he slammed the box of garbage into the pit behind the house. He kicked it hard just for good measure.

David had come around a couple times and Evan carefully avoided him. The last thing he needed was to hear how Mr. Indian Prince was spending his time having tea and crumpets with the town's old biddies. He didn't care if he ever saw that pretty-boy face again. Well, maybe just to throw a dirt clod at it to see if dirt would even stick.

He picked up a heavy hand-sized rock and threw it at the garbage pile as hard as he could. The satisfying sound of glass breaking cheered him up briefly.

He missed Morgan, though. He hadn't been to town since Evan blurted out the stuff about Wounded Knee. Nobody had seen hide nor hair of him. Of course, Evan was probably the only one who missed the old coot. James was too busy telling stories with that drunken Colton guy and his friends to even notice that Morgan hadn't been around. And David was too busy playing Indian prince. And all the other idiots in town were too stupid to even try to get to know Morgan.

He threw another rock into the garbage pit and was disappointed not to hear any glass shattering.

His dissatisfaction stemmed in large part from what went on at the store every night. Colton and his drunk cowboys would sit at the back bar with James telling stupid stories. According to Colton, he'd been just about everywhere and done just about everything. He sounded like a character out of a dime novel. Actually, he sounded more like he was all the characters out of all of the dime novels. Being in the same room with the great hunters continued to make Evan angry and irritated, but he couldn't stay away. Every night he was drawn in, sitting alone until Terrel joined him. The reporter would usually start with the Colton bunch and then join Evan in the corner by the little checkers table.

At first Colton, always hungry for attention, would holler over to Terrel to make sure he was listening to every story. Terrel would smile and pretend he was scribbling on an invisible pad. After a while, Colton gave up, grumbled about small-town reporters and continued spinning tall tales for his thirsty friends.

"I'm not so sure that blowhard has ever been west of Ohio before last month," Terrel had muttered to Evan.

Since few adults talked to Evan in such a confidential way, he began to like the young reporter from Sioux Falls. Oh sure, he liked to show off and act like a big, important reporter, but after getting to know him better, Evan thought he was mostly a good guy. When he stopped trying to impress people, he was actually pretty impressive himself.

Terrel seemed to enjoy talking to Evan and to be genuinely interested in his exploits in the Badlands. Terrel also understood that much of James's shifting rendition of the incident was hot air. Terrel said Evan's story would be a good sidebar to his "feature article" once someone shot the sheep.

"The reason this is such a big story is it reflects a change of times," Terrel said authoritatively. "With T.R. in the White House, there is more appreciation for the wild things. He's even starting to set aside some areas as 'national parks' to preserve them. Maybe he'll come out here and hunt the sheep himself. He's an accomplished big game hunter, you know.

"The time of conquering Mother Nature may be ending. I even did a story on a guy up north who's raising a herd of buffalo," he said loudly, looking around to see if anyone else was listening.

Evan had never seen a buffalo. Years ago, they had roamed the plains by the millions, but they'd been hunted nearly out of existence.

Terrel said a man named Scotty Phillips was raising a small herd up in the Missouri Breaks. He was letting them pasture instead of putting them in a zoo and was going to keep raising them like cattle. Terrel said they were about the only buffalo left in the world.

Evan picked up another rock and chucked it at the garbage pile, listening for another bottle to break. "Missed again, damn it," he grumbled to himself. He was missing everything. He didn't get to hunt the sheep. He didn't get to see the buffalo. He was stuck here in town taking out the garbage.

With all the stupid chores his father had given him, he never had a chance to get out in the Badlands. Every night he had to listen to Colton and the other great hunters tell stories about the famous hunt for the ram as they drank whiskey with James. It didn't sound like any of them had the foggiest notion of where to go or what to do out there. Colton had hired some old guy from Deadwood who had never even been to the Badlands to guide the Lauper party. The parade through town as the Lauper party left for their daily hunt grated on Evan so much he stayed in the house every morning.

"You can't sit out here throwing rocks at the garbage forever," a cheerful voice said from behind him. His mother had stepped out of the back door of the house. "Why don't you come in and have a cookie and a glass of milk?" She was smiling.

"Mom, darn it, I'm not a kid," he said, but he followed her inside anyway and slid into a seat at the little table in the kitchen.

"There sure are a lot of hunters headed out to the Badlands." She took a pitcher of milk out of the icebox and poured a glass for Evan.

"They go out there, but they don't know where to look," Evan said with disgust, his mouth half-filled with one of her fresh-baked oatmeal cookies. "Even the fancy guys who hired guides aren't seeing any sign of the sheep."

"Evan, don't talk with your mouth full." She joined him at the table, picked up a large cookie and took a small bite. "I, for one will be glad when the whole thing blows over."

Evan always thought it was funny that his Mom took such small bites of cookies and other treats but still ate as much as he did. "Have you talked with David at all?" she asked as she dabbed at the corners of her mouth with her apron.

"No, he's too busy having tea and such," Evan said without as much acid in his voice as he thought he'd have. "I'll see him sometime this summer, I reckon."

His mom smiled showing her dimples. "From what I saw at the gathering yesterday at the Jones's, David would much rather be cavorting around with you than showing off for Mrs. Blake." She ducked her head and looked toward the open window. "But don't you go telling anyone I said that," she whispered. She laughed lightly in spite of herself.

Evan smiled broadly. She wiped her mouth again neatly with her apron and folded her half-eaten cookie in a towel. She never ate very much in front of the men. Evan was tempted to see if he could steal it when she wasn't looking. With a mother's sense for mischief, she slipped the cookie in the pocket of her apron and smiled at him. "Now, why don't you go out for the day and find your friends? I'll cover the store."

Evan started to jump up and hug her, but then remembered that he was almost fourteen. He felt a little guilty about plotting to steal her cookie. "Ummm, thanks Mom, but Pa wanted me to clean out the back shed, sweep the floor and make some space for the new stock coming in. I betteeeeerrrr . . ." He looked at her sideways with raised eyebrows.

"You let me deal with your father, Evan," she said. "That damned shed has been a mess for over a year now and it doesn't need to be cleaned up today." Evan beamed as she shooed him toward the door. "Now scoot. I don't want to see your dirty face around the store today."

Evan jumped up and in spite of himself gave her a quick kiss on the cheek. He let out a short whoop and felt like kicking up his heels as he burst out the back door, carefully avoiding the store and his father.

The morning sun felt wonderful on his face, and he felt better than he had in days. It was like a huge weight had been removed from his shoulders. He had nothing to do all day but play. It was like the old days, except that he didn't have anyone to play with.

Two horses pulling a wagon were clattering through town fast, raising a cloud of dust. Evan quickly moved out of the street and stood back against the front of the Johnsons's house. As the wagon got closer he saw Edmund Blake driving the team much faster than his normal plodding pace. His black suit was dusty and disheveled and he'd lost his hat.

Evan was shocked. He'd never seen Edmund move otherwise than slowly and elegantly.

Emily Johnson startled him by opening the door right behind him. "Sorry, Emily," Evan stuttered. "I was just trying to get out of the road! Mr. Blake didn't even see me."

"I reckon he's headed up to Kadoka and the telegraph." Emily said in her screechy voice, swishing her dark blue skirt softly. She tilted her head seductively, as if begging him to ask her more.

"Telegraph?" Evan wrinkled his brow. Getting or sending telegraphs was an unusual event in Interior. "What's he got to send a telegraph for?"

Emily looked off into the distance, her green eyes glittering. "Well, I don't know if I should tell . . ." She let her voice tail off softly.

Evan let out an exasperated sigh. In the last few years Emily had gone from being a hand-waving know-it-all to an attention-craving tease. Some days she seemed like a real person and he enjoyed being around her. She could almost be a friend if she wasn't a girl. Then on other days she'd act like a complete idiot and get mad at him all the time for no reason.

"Just tell me what's going on," Evan said in a voice he forced to be calm. "Or I'll go ask someone else." He started to turn away.

Emily's small mouth formed into a pout. "Well if you must know, David's Injun father showed up at the Blakes's house last night." Her shrill voice rose even higher than normal.

"Stone Eagle? At the Blakes'?" Evan turned to face her.

"David and Mr. Blake weren't home," she said in her know-it-all tone, grabbing Evan's arm. "My mom said he nearly scared Mrs. Blake to death."

"What did he want?" Evan asked, backing out of reach of her grasp.

"Well, I'm getting to that." She straightening up and whipped her blonde hair around and over her shoulder. "Evan Warner, you always want to hurry, hurry, hurry."

Evan shuffled his feet and scraped the top of his boot along the rock foundation of the house. "What. Did. He. *Want?*" He slowly enunciated each syllable.

"My mom said Mrs. Blake slammed the door right in his face," she said with a broad sweep of her hand to simulate the slamming. "And my pa said that she probably scared that damn Injun more than he scared her." She giggled and covered her mouth with her hand.

"What's Mr. Blake gonna do?" Evan asked, again trying to restrain himself. Getting information from Emily was exasperating, but she was the only person he could talk to right now.

"He was down here this morning looking for Morgan, but ain't nobody seen him in days. It's too far to go all the way out to his ranch, so Mr. Blake was going to telegraph for help."

"Why does he need help? Did Stone Eagle do anything?" Evan persisted, searching the blonde girl's face.

"I'm getting there. If you would just be more patient, Evan Warner, people would talk to you more." She held up a hand to his chest. Although more chatter from Emily Johnson was something he could usually do without, he kept his mouth shut. "My pa said he's afraid the Injun wants more money or wants to see David. Mr. and Mrs. Blake want him run out of this part of the country before David ever hears about him. My mom said they're afraid David will run off and go back to being a heathen savage or something."

It didn't seem right to Evan to not tell David, but it was none of his business, David being a prince and all.

He opened his mouth to ask another question, but Emily said. "I don't think David would run off and be a savage at all. He isn't really an Injun. He talks so nice. But my pa thinks so. He said that once a dirty Injun, always a dirty Injun and new clothes and fancy talk don't . . ."

Evan had heard quite enough of Emily's chatter. It was his fault that Morgan wasn't around to calm everyone down. Him and his big mouth. He wondered if the old rancher would ever come to town again.

He needed to see Morgan right away, even if he was still mad. His mother and father wouldn't be happy about it, but he was going out to Morgan's ranch. He turned his back on Emily abruptly and started home to pack up.

"Evan Warner, you are just the rudest boy ever," Emily yelled after him, her screeching voice hitting a new level. "I'm never going to tell you anything ever ahhh-gain!" The last words he heard from were in a sweeter tone, "Tell David 'hi' if you see him!"

Sure, I won't, Evan thought as he sneaked around behind the store to the house. He needed to pick up his canteen and some food. It was a good three-hour hike out to Morgan's place, even with the shortcuts.

Luckily, his mom wasn't in the house, so he didn't have to explain anything to her. He found his canteen, grabbed a chicken leg and a wing from the icebox and wrapped them in a handkerchief in his bag. He slammed his hat low over his eyes and scribbled a note to his mom telling her he'd be camping in the Badlands and wouldn't be back until tomorrow.

Now if he could just sneak by the store without his father hearing him, he could be on his way.

He slid out the back door and to the window on the side of the store to see where his father was. He heard his mother and father in an animated conversation.

Evan knew it wasn't right, but if he stayed right where he was, he could hear almost everything that was said through the open window without being seen. He didn't move.

"You did what!" his father yelled. Evan couldn't help but peek around through the open window. Even through the gloom of the store Evan could see his face was very red. "I have work for that boy here."

His mom spoke in a voice Evan thought was reserved for him when he really made a mess of things. "You don't have any work that can't wait," she scolded. "I know what you're trying to do. You're trying to make sure he doesn't go out and find that damned sheep without you."

"I certainly am not," his father said angrily from behind the counter. "He's just a boy. He couldn't shoot that sheep—"

"You and I both know he's a better tracker than most men in this town, including you," she interrupted. She pointed her thin finger at her husband. "James, that boy isn't a child anymore. He's on his way to becoming a man. The sooner you understand that, the better off we'll all be."

"Ah, hell! That kid opens his mouth and just about anything spills out." His father wiped the countertop furiously.

"James, he's thirteen. It sounded like he was all of a man when he rescued you."

Through the little window Evan watched his father lower his head and take a deep breath. "He did good out there, I know. Most of the time, though, he just doesn't pay any attention to what he says or does." He shook his head. "I just can't believe how goddamned stupid he is sometimes. Everyone thinks so."

"Evan is not *stupid*!" His mother slammed her hand on the counter with a resounding *whack!*

Evan had heard enough and started down the street as fast as he could go. He couldn't believe his father said he was stupid. *I shoulda' left him out in the Badlands,* he thought.

He had to get out of this damned town and away from his damned father. He was so distracted that he barely noticed a familiar voice shouting his name. He didn't feel like talking to anyone so he kept his head down and kept walking toward the outskirts of town and the Badlands.

A small rock caught him in the back right between the shoulder blades. It startled him and he spun around to see David's smiling face ten feet away. *Great,* he thought. *This is the last thing I need. The prince probably thinks I'm stupid, too.*

"I guess it takes a rock to slow you down," David said, gaving him his trademark smile. "I've been trying to catch up to you all week."

"I'm probably too stupid to know how to talk," Evan snapped. "And throwing rocks at a person ain't nice."

David's smile faded. "What's wrong with you? I was just foolin'. Sorry I hit you. I was just trying to get your attention."

Evan smiled in spite of himself. David looked a little more like the kid he used to be. "It's okay," Evan said as he kicked at the dirt in the road. He looked at David out of the corner of his eye. "You always threw like a girl anyway."

"Why you . . ." David stuttered in mock anger and jumped at Evan, knocking him down into the dust of the road. Evan whooped and pulled the Indian boy down with him. They rolled in the dust cursing and laughing at the same time, forgetting that they were thirteen.

After a few minutes of wrestling they stopped and the dust started to settle in the morning sun. Breathing hard, Evan rolled off David and landed on his back. "And you can't wrestle worth a damned either." With a war whoop, David jumped back on him, pinning his shoulders to the ground. Both boys were laughing so hard they thought their sides would burst.

Evan finally rolled off and they sat side by side in the dust by the side of the road. He looked over at the dirt covering David's face and suit. For the first time in two years, he was actually seeing David again. "Whew, is Mrs. Blake gonna be mad at you," he snickered.

David wiped some of the dusty sweat from his forehead. "And what about you, dirt pig? Your mom's gonna be washing for a week!"

Remembering what he needed to do, Evan's expression suddenly turned sober. "I'm going out to Morgan's. He won't care if I'm dirty." Then, almost under his breath, he added, "That is, if he'll talk to me."

"What's going on?" David asked, looking into Evan's face. "You walked right past me. And now you're off to find Morgan?"

Evan's anger and frustration flared to the surface. "Oh, everything is all messed up. My pa thinks I'm stupid and just orders me around all the time," he fumed. "I'm damn sick of him and his drunken hunters mouthing off about the sheep all the time."

"Why'd your father call you stupid?" David asked, vigorously brushing the dust off his clothes. "What'd you do?"

"I didn't do nothin'." Evan shook his head and spit into the dust in the road. "He just thinks that."

"Evan, you're anything but stupid. You're just smart in ways some folks don't understand or appreciate." David slapped his thigh so the dust made a little cloud. "Why don't you and I go down to the creek and go fishing or something. To hell with your father. To hell with tea parties. To hell with all the adults."

The offer was tempting, but Evan knew he couldn't go fishing. "Thanks," he replied. "Maybe another time, but I really have to see Morgan." He took off one boot and emptied the dirt out of it.

"I wish I could go out with you, but things are all crazy around here," David said with a grimace. "Mr. and Mrs. Blake are always whispering and distracted. They stop talking as soon as I come into the room. They were driving me crazy and I had to get out of the house. She wants me back in half an hour. It's like they don't want me around but they don't want me to go anywhere. What do you think is going on?"

Evan remained silent and continued emptying the dirt from his boots. David watched him closely, and suddenly grabbed him by the arm.

"You know something!" he said, looking Evan straight in the face. "Evan, I've known you long enough to tell when you have something to say."

Evan took a deep breath and looking up from his boots, said, "David, your pa is back in town." "Stone Eagle. He went to the door at your house yesterday and scared Mrs. Blake."

Evan searched David's face but saw no reaction. His face was as still as a statue. After a pause, he spoke forcefully, saying, "Everybody keeps telling me what I am. The Blakes, the school, that man, the voices in my dream . . ." His voice trailed off and his eyes were looking into the distance.

"What dream? What voices?" Evan asked.

David shook his head. "Never mind."

"Mr. Blake was going to send a telegram or something," Evan said quickly. "At least that's what Emily Johnson said. I was going to tell Morgan. He'll know what to do."

"Do? There's nothing to do," David said with irritation. He rubbed his knuckles. "I can't believe nobody told me he went to the house."

"I think they were scared you'd be scared or run off or something," Evan said, his voice fading off as he realized how this must sound to his friend.

Abruptly, David got up. He seemed to have aged several years in the last twenty seconds. "You go see Morgan," he said firmly. "I'll handle the Blakes." He reached out a hand to help Evan up out of the dust. As the boys' eyes drew level he added, "and everything else."

"Evan," David said, putting his hands on Evan's shoulders. "We're not our fathers. Neither of us are."

Evan started to say he didn't understand what David meant, but before he could talk, David slapped him on the back. "Say hello to Morgan for me and tell him not to worry, I'll have things under control here in town." He turned and walked toward the middle of town.

Evan raised his hand in a goodbye wave to David's back. He thought David looked like a grown man as he walked purposefully down the street, shoulders high, hands in his pockets and eyes staring straight ahead. He was surprised when instead of heading for home, David turned into the store.

Evan took a deep breath and brushed more of the dust off his clothes. His father would probably think David was stupid too, but Evan couldn't worry about that now. He needed to see Morgan. The sooner he got out of town and away from all these people, the better.

Chapter Twelve

M ORGAN'S RANCH WAS on the north side of the Badlands and Interior was on the southeastern edge. It was going to be a long trek, but Evan was prepared.

As he climbed around the first spire of the Badlands and left the town behind him, Evan felt better with every step. By the time he got down into the first dry wash and felt the warm, loose sand along the bottom through his boots, the problems back in town seemed far away and trivial. Out here nobody cared if you were a boy or a man, an Indian or white, or part of the future or the past. The Badlands had been here for millions of years and would be here for another million.

North of the Badlands, the flat plains of Dakota stretched far out of sight. The plains dropped abruptly a hundred feet into the Badlands's jumble of spires, plateaus and washes. The early settlers called this drop the Wall, and the name stuck.

Morgan had settled on the prairie that ran along the top of the Wall. His claim included some of the most beautiful vistas in the west. When the rain came at the right time, the top of the Wall turned emerald green against the gray-brown clay of the Badlands. With the winds and uncertain rain, the land wasn't ideal for producing the grass to raise cattle, but Morgan always managed to survive.

The three hours passed quickly. Evan knew where he was going and moved with confidence through the intricate maze. As he climbed the trail up to the top of the Wall toward Morgan's place he wondered what he'd find. He could ignore what Mrs. Blake or the Johnsons or even his father and mother thought about him, but he couldn't bear to disappoint Morgan. In the past, when Morgan got angry or frustrated with Evan, he would give him a silent, deadly look, maybe a mutter or a curse, and it would blow over. But he'd never upset Morgan in front of anyone like he did by bringing up Wounded Knee that night in the store.

As he neared the top of the Wall, his feet felt heavier, but not just from the exertion of the climb. He'd practiced what he was going to say a hundred times in the last couple of days and established arguments based on every possible response Morgan could put forth. He just had to make him understand he didn't mean any harm. The words had just come out.

At least it'd be good to see the fine green pasture in front of Morgan's soddy again. Most settlers had abandoned sod cabins as wood had become more available, but Morgan had stuck with tradition. Like the cabins the first settlers had built, Morgan's backed up into a small rise and had a roof made of firm prairie sod.

As he cleared the top of the trail, Evan was startled to see Morgan standing there waiting for him. His hat was pulled low over his weathered face. He looked older than Evan remembered.

"Um, hi Morgan," Evan began in a hesitant voice. He'd known exactly what he was going to say and practiced it over and over. Now he couldn't remember any of it. Words came tumbling out of his mouth, wrestling with each other. "Morgan, I'm so sorry. I didn't mean to make you mad. It just blurted out," he said.

Morgan said nothing. He just stared at Evan, his eyes barely visible beneath the brim of his hat. The silence sucked the oxygen out of the air.

Finally, Morgan spoke. "Evan, when you was a boy you could get by sayin' whatever came to mind." His voice was low and reminded Evan of an old creaking door. The words flowed over him like they were spoken by the Badlands themselves. "But as you become a man, you have to realize that you can hurt people. There ain't nobody responsible for your mouth but you. You can't just say you're sorry and make it go away. Man's gotta live with all the things he says and all the things he does. You can be as sorry as you want, and you can make up for it all you want, but you always gotta live what has happened."

Evan felt his stomach drop. Was Morgan going to send him back home? "Morgan, I know I did wrong, but it was that Colton guy talking all big and—"

Morgan held a hand up silencing him. "When a man makes a mistake, he admits it, does what he can to make it good and puts it behind him. He don't make no excuses. He lives with himself and goes on."

Evan stood uncomfortably in silence, scraping at a small tuft of prairie grass with his boot. He felt so small, like such a little kid. He wished there was a hole to crawl into. Morgan watched him silently for a while from beneath the brim of his hat.

Finally, the old rancher's face broke into a smile. He reached a hand out and clapped Evan on the shoulder. "You never could control that mouth of yours, boy, but it sure is good to see you," he said, his voice lighter. "Let's go get you some dinner."

Relief washed over Evan's body and made his knees weak. His shoulders dropped and his cheeks seemed to sag. He realized that he'd been holding his breath. A smile, his first in a long time, came to his face as he walked with Morgan back to the soddy. "Thanks, Morgan. I'd like that," he said, fighting against a catch in his throat. He didn't dare cry in front of Morgan.

They walked side-by-side through the prairie grass toward the soddy, enjoying the silence. Evan saw Morgan's small herd of cattle grazing off to the west and old Blue in his corral behind the cabin. The setting sun gave a golden hue to the gray-green of the prairie.

On the horizon, two riders emerged from the shadows behind one of the rolling hills a quarter-mile away. They rode unhurriedly into the golden light toward the small ranch. Evan could only make out their outlines against the setting sun but it was clear that they were Indian riders. And they weren't dressed in reservation clothes.

"Morgan," he said in an urgent tone, pulling on the old rancher's arm. "Look!"

Morgan stopped walking and looked toward the dark figures of the riders. He stood silently with his hands at his sides and face to the sun, ignoring the squirming of the boy next to him.

As they reached Morgan's herd of cattle, the two riders slowed and approached a yearling. One of the riders dropped what looked to be a rope around the young cow's head and turned around. The other rider looked toward Morgan, creating a perfect silhouette in the gold of the setting sun.

Morgan waved broadly at the rider. The man didn't wave back. He turned his horse and followed his companion and the cow.

"Morgan," Evan said, his voice a harsh whisper. "They're stealing that cow!"

The old rancher ignored the boy and stood still with his arm raised. Evan heard the meadowlark calls across the prairie as the riders slipped back into the shadows behind the hill with the cow. Finally Morgan lowered his arm and looked over at him. "You got a real talent for the obvious, boy," he said matter-of-factly.

Evan felt his heart thumping and he was breathing hard from the excitement. "You let them steal from you? Who are they? Why didn't you . . ."

Morgan put one arm around Evan's shoulders and let out a dry laugh that sounded like a cough. "Now what did I just tell you about keeping your mouth shut sometimes?"

"Morgan," he said, looking over at the rancher. "They didn't even wave thanks."

"Yeah, boy, I know."

Morgan dropped his arm from around his shoulders and they went on toward the sod cabin, their feet crackling on the dry grass. The sun was dropping quickly now, turning the golden sky to dark red.

Morgan pointed to an old fire pit, "Split that log over there and I'll get us some supper."

The fire pit was about a yard across, ringed with head-sized rocks charred black. It was filled with feather-light white ash from the fires of many nights. There were none of the ugly, black, half-burned logs that filled most fire pits. Everything had been burned completely. Around the pit were two large cottonwood logs with the bark stripped clean. One was stained and chipped like it was used every night. The other was gray with age but looked mostly unused.

Around the pit the ground was covered with bark from split logs. As Evan approached the gray, scarred chopping block, his feet sank into a spongy carpet of bark several inches deep. The head of the axe he pulled from the block had no paint on it and was dirty and chipped, but the blade was filed clean and silver and sharp. The hard, smooth wood of the handle felt good in his hands. He wiggled the axe head to make sure it wasn't loose like the one at home. There was no movement and it had a firm, well-used feel.

Evan went to work chopping the logs piled behind him. As he started his swing the axe head felt heavy, heavier than any axe he'd ever used. When he brought it down on the center of the log, it aggressively bit into the wood with a loud *thwack*. He smiled as the log fell into two even pieces. He continued to split the sawcut logs that had been stacked neatly behind the chopping block.

He was so intent on splitting, he didn't hear Morgan come out of the sod hut and stand by the fire pit. "We ain't gonna have a forest fire, boy. You done split enough."

Evan laughed. "It's way easier to split this stuff than what we have back home."

"That's probably because you ain't sharpened your axe in ten years," Morgan said in his deep, rumbling voice. "You do stuff right the first time, it makes it easier down the road."

Evan nodded and watched the old rancher quickly put together a small tepee of kindling for the fire and strike a flint to start it. In just a few minutes, he had a small fire burning very hot. Morgan put an old black-covered pot on the rock in the middle of the pit. "We'll boil some water for tea until we get a cookin' fire," he said.

Almost everyone Evan knew would start cooking their meat as soon as the fire gave off the slightest amount of heat. It was no wonder the meat was always nearly raw or burnt or both.

Morgan slowly slid onto the well-worn cottonwood log, stretching his legs in front of him. "So, what's been goin' on in town the last few days?" he asked, pointing to the log on the other side of the pit.

Evan had felt so at ease with Morgan he had completely forgotten about town. It seemed like a million miles away. "Gosh, Morgan, I forgot to tell you that Mr. Blake was looking for you," he said as he sat on the log. "Stone Eagle was back in town."

Morgan looked up sharply. "Where?" he asked, his voice harsher than usual.

"Emily Johnson said her ma told her that Stone Eagle went to the Blakes's house. Mrs. Blake answered the door and slammed it in his face," Evan said without taking a breath. "Mr. Blake and David weren't home and she was scared to death."

"Anyone else see him or talk to him?"

"No," Evan said, shaking his head. "Not that I heard. She just slammed the door and he left, I guess."

Morgan seemed to relax as he smiled slightly and leaned back. "That ol' battle axe probably scared him more than he scared her," he said absently, moving some of the kindling around the fire. "Still, I better get to town before things get all blowed up. I gotta get those cattle outta the west forty tomorrow but then I'll go in."

"I can help you tomorrow, Morgan," Evan said, looking up at the old rancher eagerly. "My folks know I'm here . . . sorta."

"If'n you can give me a hand tomorrow we can get into town tomorrow night or the next mornin," Morgan said as he used a stick to stir the fire again and take the lid off the pot. "You sure your ma is okay with you stayin' out here a couple o' days?"

Evan nodded without speaking.

Morgan scooped out a cup of water and poured it into two tin cups beside him on the log. He carefully dipped a cloth packet into each cup. The scent of sage wafted into the air. "Damn, I hope that Blake woman doesn't get everyone all riled up," he said as he steeped the tea.

As he accepted a cup of sage tea, Evan thought about how much more relaxed and at home Morgan seemed around the fire than when he came in to visit the store. He held the hot liquid to his lips and smelled the light sage aroma mixed with the smell of the cooking fire.

They sat in silence for a while sipping tea and watching the fire as darkness started to close in on the prairie. Without looking away from the fire Evan said, "And my pa thinks I'm stupid."

Although he could feel Morgan's eyes on him, Evan kept his focus on the small flickering flames. Finally, he heard a wheezing sound like air through a bellows. He looked up and saw the old rancher break out into an outright laugh, slapping his hand on his thigh. "It's not funny," Evan said indignantly. "I heard him say so to my mom."

"I'm sorry, boy," Morgan said wiping his eye with a finger. "The thought of James Warner thinking you are stupid is the damned funniest thing I've heard in years, and the thought that you are upset by it is even funnier. All fathers think their kids are stupid, 'specially when they start to become adults." Morgan stretched with his arms over his head like his stomach muscles were sore.

Evan looked at him bewildered. "But I heard him say it," he said in a small voice. He didn't know what he expected Morgan's reaction would be, but he did know it wasn't laughter.

Morgan sat up straight on the log and pointed with his cup in his hand. "Did he say it to you, boy?"

"No, I heard him saying it to my mom. Well, ummm . . . I kind of overheard it," The toes of his boots looked very interesting to Evan all of a sudden.

"You gotta understand, boy, that when things don't go right with a man, he lashes out at whatever is closest to him. James is a good man and a friend of mine. But he damned near got hisself killed on that ledge last week. He was damned lucky you were there, and don't think he don't know it." Morgan's voice carried out into the darkness of the prairie.

"He never said nothin' to me about bein' lucky I was there," Evan mumbled, feeling a little sheepish and small.

"You ever thought your pa was stupid?" Morgan abruptly asked.

"Well yeah, I guess so."

"You ever tell someone—like David?"

"Yeah, I guess I did." He looked over at the old rancher out of the corner of his eye.

"You ever tell your pa to his face?" Without waiting for an answer he continued, "No, because you didn't want to hurt his feelings."

Evan looked down at the ground between his boots. "Guess that's true. But he's a parent and he isn't supposed to say stuff like that about me."

Morgan looked down toward the fire, the light giving a red-yellow glow to his craggy face. "The closer you get to bein' a man, the more you will understand there ain't nobody that's perfect. Ain't nobody free of mistakes—not your pa, not you, not me."

Morgan poked at the fire with his stick. "All you can do is the best you can do. When you make mistakes, you stand up and take your punishment like a man and make no excuses."

The crackling of the fire was the only sound breaking the stillness of the prairie.

"So when will I be a man, Morgan, so they stop treating me like a kid?" He took another sip of tea, slurping loudly.

Morgan laughed his dry coughing laugh again. "Part of you is a man right now, the part that drug your old man off that ledge." He looked up and his eyes met Evan's. "And part of you is a dumb-assed kid who talks too much." Morgan laughed again and threw his stick at him, bouncing off his shoulder.

"The important part is for you to know which parts is which," Morgan said smiling broadly. "That dumb-assed kid will always be a part of you, at least I hope so."

Evan could not help but smile. What had seemed like such a huge weight upon his mind in town was pretty minor out here.

"I've had enough talkin'," Morgan declared, and he uncovered a cast iron frying pan with two big steaks in it. "It's time we got to cookin'."

Evan watched as Morgan's practiced hand put the pan on the fire. As he prepared the meat he told Evan what the cuts of the meat were, how they were cut and how to tell if the fire was at the right heat.

He surprised Evan by pulling a small wooden box out of his bag. The lid and the sides of the box were dark with age and smudges of soot and dirt. He carefully set the box down on a flat spot on the log beside him. He pulled off the lid and set it beside the box in a precise manner, revealing a gleaming white lace handkerchief. He carefully pulled at the folded corners of the handkerchief, using only his finger tips, to unwrap a set of pewter salt and pepper shakers. The firelight danced off their silver sheen. He gently lifted them out of the box one at a time and lightly seasoned the meat. His eyes never left the shakers as he carefully rewrapped them with the handkerchief, replaced them in the box and slid the dirty wooden box back into his bag.

Evan started to ask about the wooden box, but remembered

what Morgan told him about shutting his mouth sometimes. He let the smells of the fire and the steaks flow over him.

"No matter what you think of your ma and pa, they're the only ones you got," he said looking up at Evan again, the firelight glittering in his eyes. "You don't choose family. You accept them for what they are and be darn grateful to have them." He patted the top of bag where he'd put the box and returned his focus to the fire.

When the meat had finished cooking Morgan slid each of the steaks onto a tin plate and handed one to Evan, along with a knife and fork. The hot, rare steak nearly melted in his mouth.

"So what's goin' on with your great sheep hunt?" Morgan asked through a mouthful of red meat. A drop of juice on his chin glistened in the firelight.

Evan was surprised that he had forgotten so much of what had seemed so important only a few hours ago. "Well, nobody has seen any sign of the ram. There are a couple of big shot guys from back east and a bunch of ordinary guys huntin' every day." He waved his fork in the air. "The biggest guy is an Englishman named Lauper. He has a big camp on the outside of town. They say his tents are nicer'n most people's houses."

Evan took a gulp of tea from his tin cup. "He's been hiring guys to take him out to the Badlands and guide him to the ram, but nobody is doin' any good. He has this big guy in buckskins named Colton who's his main guide." Evan's voice took on a bitter edge. "He comes into town every night to drink whiskey, tell stories and brag about stuff with the other hunters and my pa."

Morgan slowed his chewing. "Guy with the big mustache and bigger mouth that we saw the last time I was in town?"

Evan laughed, coughing and almost choking on a bite of steak. "The mouth, yes. That's definitely him."

"He ain't gonna find no sheep unless somebody leads him right to it," Morgan said as he shook his head.

"They hired some guy named Butch, but I heard he didn't do so good. Colton told my pa they were going to fire him." Evan hesitated and then said, "Colton told my pa that they'd hire him to guide 'em if his leg wasn't all gummed up."

Morgan laughed out loud. "James Warner as a huntin' guide. I'd pay to see that," he cackled, slapping his knee. "Sounds like they're getting pretty desperate."

"Colton told Pa that Lauper didn't think the Badlands was gonna be so tough. Said he had been to Africa and South America huntin', but never out where there wasn't no water and to where the terrain was so hard to move in." He smiled a little and wiped the grease out of the corner of his mouth with his sleeve. "They don't know how to get around out there so it sounds like they're wanderin' in circles most of the time."

Morgan looked over at the boy and pointed at him with his knife. "You know the Badlands pretty much better than anyone. Why don't you guide him?"

There was silence, except for the crackle of the fire as Evan scraped his boot against the rocks on the fire pit. "I'm not sure. Probably more money that I'd see in years, but it just don't seem right, somehow."

He looked up at Morgan. "I figured David and me was gonna find the ram, but that didn't work out at all. I still want to be the one to find him, but now I'm not sure why."

The fire crackled and popped, sending a shower of sparks into the night air. It glowed brighter as the sunset faded into ever-darkening gray. Morgan stopped eating and closely considered Evan. Finally, he grinned and said in a slow drawl, "You are startin' to grow up, boy."

Evan felt as warm and good inside as he had in a long time. He watched the bright red embers of the fire pulsing as if they were alive and felt them drawing the tension out of him. It felt good to belong.

Quietly he asked, "Morgan, what really did happen at Wounded Knee?"

They sat in silence for several minutes, only this time Evan felt relaxed and time didn't seem to go so slowly. The silence was part of this place. Morgan pulled out his watch and looked at it, but couldn't have seen much in the flickering firelight. He slowly returned it to his pocket.

Finally, he began to speak in a far-away tone Evan had never heard him use before.

"It was like I told ya the other day, we was wintering in Fort Sully, lookin' for an easy time of it. Call came down to go to the Red Cloud agency. They said they didn't want Big Foot's band to link up with the Ghost Dancers at the Stronghold in the Badlands.

"We spent three days chasin' them around through that cold bitch of a prairie. Finally, they just seemed to run out of the will to go on. They stopped in a gully of Wounded Knee Creek. The banks were pretty high on both sides and the floor leveled out to about fifty yards wide. Then it narrowed the further down you got until it was just twenty yards across.

"Lieutenant Baker told us to set up our Hotchkiss guns on the bank where the ravine narrowed. That way if anybody come down the ravine we could stop them. There were two other Hotchkisses up further on the high ground around the main camp."

Morgan looked up, the firelight flickering off his face and said, "I'm telling you, boy, that damned heavy thing was cold. Just touching the gun barrel 'bout froze your fingers off. Baymaker, my partner, was holding the ammo for me and cussin' up a blue streak."

The story must have lived inside Morgan for a long time. Now that he was letting it out, it was like a horse that had been cooped up in a stall for too long. The first steps into the light were slow and tentative, but soon the old rancher's voice gained strength as he continued. His voice became strong and clear.

"Way up the draw we could see the officers talking with Big Foot and his band. The Indians were all crowded around, 'most of three hundred of them. The warriors were up front and the squaws were hangin' to the back carrying the kids. We never thought there would be women and kids when we got dispatched from Sully."

Morgan looked up from the fire at Evan and paused. "I'm telling you, we never knew there was gonna be no women and kids." Evan nodded but said nothing. The old rancher turned back to stare into the flames flickering at the edges of the embers.

"I don't know what the officers and Injuns were jawing about but there was lots of yellin' and arm-wavin'. Finally, we could see ol' Big

Foot pull out this big ol' rifle and throw it on the ground. He turned to holler something to the other Injuns and a few more threw their guns on the ground.

"Baymaker looked at me with that dirty-toothed grin of his. 'Don't look like there is gonna be a fight after all,' he said. 'Looks like old Big Foot done give up. Damn, I wish we could'a got in an Injun Fight.' Biggest goddamned fool in the army, he was.

"We could still see the group of Injuns milling around and a few of them throwing their guns in a pile. Must not have been fast enough for the officers because one of 'em was yellin' something to Big Foot and a-wavin' his arms."

Morgan paused and put his hands out in front of him, fingers splayed, and said, "Then there was the crack of a shot. I don't know where it came from or who shot it but it was somewhere up the valley. I remember that I was lookin' down at Baymaker's fat face, getting ready to tell him to shut his trap when we heard the shot. The look on his chubby cheeks just froze in place. I felt my stomach churn. I looked up and everyone else seemed to be frozen in place too, like somebody took one of them photographs or something. The shot kept echoing and echoing.

"An' then all hell broke loose. I heard the other Hotchkisses opening up. Our guys were all shooting from the top of the ravine. The pile of Indians that had been standing by the officers just scattered.

"'Don't let them get away,' the lieutenant was screaming at us," Morgan waved his hands. "The infantry guys on either side of us opened up but I don't know what they were shooting at.

"The smoke from the Hotckisses and the other guns filled that valley right away. All you could see was this white smoke and a head or an arm or a foot every once in a while. All you could smell was gun powder. All you could hear was guns going off up and down the valley, pop, pop, pop.

"We didn't know if they had gotten their guns and were trying to break out. Baymaker was screaming at me to shoot. The lieutenant was screaming at me to shoot. I don't know why, but I just stood there holdin' that big bitch of a gun. I just stood there. All the guns around us were shooting, but we couldn't see nothin' in the ravine but smoke."

"I remember the lieutenant grabbing my arm and putting his nose right in my face. He had a big pimple on the left side of his nose that looked like it was going to be an ugly boil. His face was so red it blended right in and you wouldn't even know he had the pimple unless his nose was real close to you. Like it was to me."

"'They're gittin' away, Morgan, goddamn it, shoot!' he yelled. The man had the worst breath in the army.

"I saw some movement in the smoke in the ravine out of the corner of my eye. I trained the Hotchkiss at the movement and opened 'er up."

Morgan hesitated and ran a hand over his face, still looking deep into the fire. Evan saw a sheen of sweat across his brow in the firelight even though the evening had cooled.

"After the first shot, I was just soldierin'. They said shoot and I shot. I put over a hundred rounds into that smoke-filled valley in less than three minutes. The guns around me stopped, but I just keep firing into that ravine, into that smoke. The lieutenant finally had to club me over the head with the butt of his rifle and put me on the ground."

Morgan pulled up his hat and leaned over to show Evan a half-dollar sized scar on this temple. "Still carry the scar today. That was about the only good thing that damned lieutenant ever did, clubbing me in the head like that." He pulled his hat back over his forehead and turned back to the fire.

"As I was layin' on the ground with my head throbbing, I could hear moaning. I thought it was coming from me so I put my hand to my mouth but it kept on. No sounds in the valley but moaning. On and on. In a few minutes the smoke started to lift and we could see what was in that valley."

Morgan blew out a deep breath that sent sparks flying out of the fire. "On a cold winter day like that, everything seems white and gray. The snow the air, the ground, our breath . . . everything was a shade of white or a shade of gray. 'Cept that day. There were patches of bright red blood everywhere. Below where I had opened up with the Hotchkiss was a pile of bodies, twenty or thirty of them. Steam risin' off the bright red blood spots like little clouds." Evan could see that Morgan's hands were shaking.

"I tried to sit up and heard Baymaker say, 'they is all women and kids 'cept that one there that never got shot.' He started laughing, that fat slime, and we were all too numb to stop him. 'There's one Indian buck in the middle of all those women and kids and can you believe it? He never got a scratch.'"

Morgan paused, running a hand over his forehead to wipe the sweat that had gathered. "I must have killed fifteen or twenty of those women and kids myself with that ol' Hotchkiss. Those big bullets tore into their bodies and turned them into meat."

Evan watched Morgan's face carefully, unable to move or speak. Morgan continued to stare directly into the flames as a single tear wound its way down the craggy lines of his face, glittering in the firelight.

"Kin you believe they tried to give me a medal for that?" he asked bitterly. "We piled up the bodies like cordwood and put 'em in a big hole in the snow. It was too damned cold to dig.

"About half the regiment was in a state of shock like I was and the rest of them were too damned dumb to understand what we had done. They had one of those photographers out there takin' pictures of the dead Injun bodies. Why would anybody want to take a picture of a dead Injun body?" He looked up at Evan, who shook his head but said nothing.

"Took the heart right out of the Lakota. They ain't never been the same. Just wasn't any fight left in them. Ghost Dancers left the Badlands and went back to Nevada or wherever the hell they come from."

Morgan stuck out his leg and moved a log into the middle of the fire with the toe of the old boot.

"After that I wasn't much good to nobody, 'specially the army. I mustered out the next spring. I didn't have much use for people after all that. Couldn't go home. I came back out to Wounded Knee that summer. Just looked like another little ravine in the plains. 'Cept it had a big hole fulla dead Injuns.

"I homesteaded me this place up here on the Wall above the Badlands and been here ever since."

He looked up at Evan, his eyes still watery under the wide brim of his hat. "So now you know the Morgan history. 'Preciate it if you didn't blurt it out everywhere."

Evan felt very calm considering everything he had heard. It was a watchful, quiet calm. "'Course not, Morgan," he said, his voice hoarse. "So, who are those Indians that always steal your cattle?"

Morgan looked back into the flames. "Don't know. They showed up a few years after I got the ranch started and just helped themselves. Until last week when you got yourself stranded on that hillside, I never talked to them."

"Didn't you ever tell nobody that they were stealin' from you?"

"Nah," he said and shook his head. "Just never seemed important. Appears they only take what they need to eat. Seemed like the least I could do."

"Don't they ever say thank you or wave or nothin'?" Evan asked.

Morgan was silent for a long while. "Guess they don't have much to be thankful for," he said.

They sat on the logs and watched the fire in silence for another hour. The flames slowly burned down to bright red coals. As the fire cooled, dark black spots around the edges of the coals slowly devoured red embers. With a puff of wind one would bravely ignite to flame only to fade into black.

"All right if I sleep here by the fire?" Evan asked. Somehow he didn't like the thought of sleeping in the dark soddy. He wanted to be close to the Badlands.

"Good idea, boy, I think I'll join you," Morgan said, his once again his usual quiet deep drawl. "In the morning we'll get them cattle and then get to town and get things all straight."

"Okay, Morgan."

After a while he looked over at the old rancher. "Morgan," he said. "Thanks."

Morgan raised his head so the last of the firelight barely illuminated the craggy lines on his face and he nodded.

Chapter Thirteen

A ND I THINK THAT ALL men's white shirts should have separate col-
lars," Mrs. Bitteman said as she slurped from the chipped teacup.
"It shows much more elegance. Don't you think so, David?"

"Umm, yes, certainly, Mrs. Bitteman," David replied. He
cringed at the sound of her slurping and tried not to look at the nickel-
sized mole on her upper lip.

He had learned that he could make inane comments without
even thinking about them. He felt empathy more than contempt for
this woman in the worn dress as he watched her clumsily sipping tea
and expounding on fashion. At Pierceson, he'd had opportunities to
hobnob with sophisticated society women who wore fashionable clothes
and drank their tea elegantly. He had found them to be just as boring
and vacuous as the farm wives of Interior. Here, the women at least
knew they were boring and vacuous but tried hard anyway.

Whether in the city or on the prairie, they all loved a handsome
Indian kid with manners. He would flash a smile, say something polite
and they fawned over him. While he disliked playing this role, it had
served him well in the past two years. He was conditioned to accept
that women would dote on a heathen savage tamed to dress up and talk
politely, so he didn't complain.

Now in the second week of Mrs. Blake's mission to drag him to
every house west of the Missouri, he feared he was starting to believe
his own line of bull.

David hadn't seen Mr. Blake since he talked with Evan the day
before. Mrs. Blake had been furious with him for getting his clothes
dirty. Then she had maintained a stony silence when he asked about
Stone Eagle knocking at the door. "Just an unfortunate incident," she
had said, suddenly needing to busy herself with putting some dishes
away. Whenever he had asked her about his father she had told him

curtly to discuss it with Mr. Blake. "It is not the sort of topic for proper conversation," she had said, waving her hand dismissively. "Edmund takes care of all those things."

For the rest of the day she had been silent and cold to him, but not disturbed enough to miss this tea at the Johanson's. David had done everything he could think of to get out of attending. He even thought about sneaking out and joining Evan at Morgan's. Yet, he wondered if he had anything in common with Evan and Morgan anymore. Sometimes he didn't feel like he had anything in common with anyone.

The Lakota voice returned to his dreams every night now. It was telling him something about the Badlands, but he could never recall exactly what it has said when he woke. It was something about not being an eagle and a hawk at the same time. He didn't want to be either. He just wanted to be himself, but he wasn't sure who that was.

As always, Mrs. Blake wore him down and he reluctantly accompanied her. As soon as she made her official introductions and her speech about his refinement and accomplishments, he snuck off to the kitchen for some privacy. Unfortunately, Mrs. Bitteman, who did not shine in front of the other ladies, had followed him and was taking full advantage of having him all to herself.

"And the hats they are showing," she said waving her hands. "Why, I just think the feathers are atrocious."

David wanted to tell her that she needed a big hat to cover that big old ugly mole on her lip. "They do tend to be distracting," he said in a voice as smooth as silk.

God, I have to get away from this woman, he thought as she unconsciously patted her frizzy gray curls. *I'm making myself sick.*

"If you'll excuse me, I really must get back to attend to Mrs. Blake." He thought anything would be better than sitting in the kitchen watching Mrs. Bitteman primp. He made a quick bow and exited the room before she could respond.

Entering the living room, he saw through the window that Mrs. Blake and Mrs. Johanson were out on the covered front porch. He hurried to the front door before Mrs. Bitteman could catch up to him but stopped when he heard their conversation floating through the open window.

". . . and that savage was just standing there right at my front door," Mrs. Blake was explaining in a dramatic voice. "I don't know why those animals never learned to bathe. I can still smell the stench!"

"Well, what did he say?" Mrs. Johanson asked, leaning over the arm of her rocking chair.

"I'm sure I don't know. He might have mumbled something but those savages can't speak with a real tongue." She took a sip of tea. "I think it's genetics or something."

"David has a beautiful voice and speaks perfectly," Mrs. Johanson commented, leaning back in her chair.

"Yes, he does," Mrs. Blake admitted with a sly smile. "But only because Mr. Blake and I worked ceaselessly to drive the savage out of him. His school in Minneapolis has the motto, 'Kill the Indian to save the man.' However; I doubt that the savage at my front door could have been saved by any school."

All his life, David had heard this type of ignorant prejudice before, and much worse. He had practiced some of it himself. One of the great sports at the school was to make fun of the new "Rez Indians" when they showed up the first day.

Today, though, he had had enough. That was his father—his flesh and blood—and Mrs. Blake spoke about him like he was an animal. *That makes me nothing but a tamed animal,* he thought. The blood rushed to his head and his ears rang. All of the frustration he had stifled in the last few weeks, perhaps in the last few years, fought its way to the surface.

Mrs. Bitteman came out of the kitchen and said far too loudly, "Well, David, I see you haven't made it outside yet."

He knew that he absolutely couldn't look at Mrs. Bitteman's mole for another second. His body moved on its own. A kick opened the front door with a bang. He burst onto the porch and stood directly in front of Mrs. Blake, fists clenched tightly.

"David," Mrs. Blake said, startled, sloshing the tea from her cup onto her best dress. "I didn't see you there."

David bowed at the waist, very low and formally. "Mistress Blake, your humble servant and trained pet has had quite enough of this party and will now take his leave and exit the premises." His dark eyes flashed with anger as he straightened up to face her.

"David!" Mrs. Blake dropped her teacup as she started to rise, cringing as she heard it crash to the floor and break.

"And don't come looking for me you ignorant, old, white biddy," he said as his smooth, handsome face curled into a snarl.

"Wha . . . Wha . . . ?" she stammered.

David jumped over the top two stairs of the porch and ran down the road toward town. He heard Mrs. Blake yelling something at him but the sound of his heart beating rapidly filled his ears. Energy surged through his body as he fled.

The brilliant sun beat on his head. Heat engulfed him as he ran down the road. He was already sweating profusely in his stiff black suit. He tore off the coat, thrashing his arms like it had a wasp's nest in the pocket and flung it down with a flourish. His tie and collar joined the pile and he kicked dust from the road on them. He hopped on one foot as he pulled off first one black shoe and sock and then the other and threw them in the general direction of the house. The women on the porch stood in a line, silently watching his outburst in horror.

He glanced down at the pile of dark clothing in the dust beside the road and then looked back up at the house. Mrs. Blake was standing on the porch with a hand over her mouth. He looked back at the limp mound of his coat and shoes and tie and, with great drama, arched his back and spit high into the air. He watched with satisfaction as the glob of spit splattered into a perfect landing, white and mucusy on the black cloth.

Without looking back at the house he loped barefoot down the dusty road.

Once around the corner and out of sight of the house, he slowed to a walk. He immediately regretted his impulse to remove his shoes. He and Evan had shucked their shoes and run barefoot around the town for entire days at a time, but that was years ago. His feet had been cooped up in the white man's shoes for too long. He was reduced to limping gingerly after a few steps, but he couldn't go back to get his shoes now.

Warner's store was just a few hundred feet down the road. Maybe Evan could loan him some boots if he was back from Morgan's. He grinned slyly as he thought about telling him the story of his explosion, especially the high arching spit. Evan always appreciated a good spit.

There was a group of men, a wagon and several horses in front of the store. The men were speaking in angry voices. David slipped around the back of the store so he wouldn't be noticed.

He reached the small house attached to the back of the store and slid along the side of the building until he could see what was going on in front without being noticed.

Two of the cowboys he'd seen drinking with James Warner and Colton stood in front of the store holding the reins of their horses. Levi Johnson was standing next to them, confronting James Warner.

"All I'm telling you," Warner said slowly, his hands outstretched and fingers splayed, "is that someone broke in last night and stole my last two gallons of whiskey. I'll get another order in the next few days. You guys have cleaned out my supply."

The first cowboy slammed his hands against his thighs, raising small clouds of dust. Tall and rangy, he looked like he hadn't shaved in weeks. His dark black beard looked harsh and rough. "We're out there in this infernal heat all day chasing some sheep that probably don't exist and you're telling me that you don't have no whiskey?" He spit on the ground, deliberately close to James's feet. "I don't believe you. You're probably holdin' it out for yourself."

"Yeah," a short, doughy-looking cowboy in a red shirt said. "C'mon, Drager, let's go check fer ourselves." He looked to the tall man for approval and took a step toward the store.

Warner put a hand on the small man's chest and pushed him back firmly. "Store's closed, boys. We're restocking."

The small man balled up his fist and looked over his shoulder for support. Drager's teeth gleamed white against his dark beard, but he made no move to help. The pudgy cowboy's fists went to open hands immediately. "So what else did this so-called thief take, storeowner?" he scoffed, backing off.

The black-bearded man reached over his horse to tie down his saddlebags. "Come on, Bob, we'd better get back to camp or that damned Colton will fire us, too."

James leaned back against the wall. "The only thing missing was the whiskey and a loaf of bread. It was probably somebody just passin' through." He looked relieved that the situation was defusing.

Johnson spoke up, his eyes bright beneath his thick blonde eyebrows. "Had to be Injuns. Any white man woulda' taken all the valuables." He smacked his lips and ran his fingers through his big red beard. "I bet it was ol' Stone Eagle. First he attacks the Blake woman and now he's stealin' whiskey. Who knows what he'll do next?"

Drager let go of his saddlebags and turned to the red-faced man. "You mean you got an Indian in these parts attacking white women? An' now he's drinkin' our whiskey, too?"

James stepped in front of the cowboy and faced Johnson. "Levi, you know that nobody attacked anybody. I heard all he did was knock on the Blakes's door."

David could feel the tension building again as Johnson's eyes narrowed. He didn't want to lose face now that he had shot off his mouth. "All I know is that Indian was out at Blake's and shook everyone up so much that Edmund took off to the county seat. An' now that he's got some whiskey in him, ain't nobody gonna be safe from that damned Stone Eagle. He was a rough one when he was around here before. I kin tell you my woman folk aren't gonna be unprotected."

James pointed a finger at Johnson. "You don't know who took the whiskey and nobody's done anything. Blake will be back with the sheriff in a day or two and my Evan's gone out to get Morgan."

Johnson spit on the road, a long string of saliva still hanging from his red beard. "Ah, t' hell with Morgan. He's probably in with 'em. An' that kid of yours spends all his time runnin' wild with that damned fancy pants, educated Injun the Blakes brung back. They're probably all in it. That's why they all come back here at the same time. Attackin' women and stealin' whiskey. All of 'em!"

Johnson's face was as red as the pudgy cowboy's shirt and drops of sweat covered his brow. "Damn it, Edmund and Amanda shoulda just had kids of their own instead'a tryin' to educate one of them animals. As soon as they brought that damned Injun kid back, he started drawin' other Injuns here like flies. It's gonna be another uprisin', I tell you." He smacked his big fist into his palm.

"So you got a wild Injun runnin' 'round here and nobody's doin' nothin' about it?" Drager hitched up his dusty pants. "That the one with the reward, you figure?"

James spread his hands out wide palms down. "You all need to calm down. Nobody's done anything but took a little whiskey and we don't know who. Just wait until Morgan gets back."

Johnson was enjoying the audience. "Ahh, Morgan lives out in the Badlands with them most the time. He ain't gonna do nothing."

Drager, the tall dark cowboy, pulled at his reins. "I ain't waitin' for no old man to tell me what to do. We may not be able to find any goddamn sheep, but I sure as hell can run down an Injun. Bob, let's find that bastard before he attacks anyone else."

"Yeah, Drager, I bet that's the Injun bastard with the reward. Let's go find him and get a scalp before he drinks all our whiskey." The pudgy cowboy climbed on his horse, an ugly gray mare, that danced as he wiggled to get set in the saddle.

David pressed back against the side of the store to stay out of sight, his heart pounding. He jumped when right beside his ear he heard a "*pssssst!*"

He turned and was startled to be face-to-face with an Indian man.

"David, come with me," the man said, pulling on the sleeve of his white shirt. David followed him to the back of the store, out of earshot of the heated scene in front of the store.

The man turned and smiled at David. "It is not a good time to be an Indian here," he said. "Even an educated one. Maybe especially an educated one." He led David back away from the building.

"Who are you?" David asked with suspicion.

"I'm Fire Brush."

David winced as he stepped on a small rock. Fire Brush's face lit up in a smile. "Your feet have gone white on you, my friend." He took his bag off his back and pulled out a pair of worn moccasins. "Wear my spare ones."

The moccasins looked worn and comfortable, if a little too big. David felt like he ought to refuse them, but his feet were not used to the hard ground. He slid them on and fell into step beside Fire Brush, heels swinging free in the borrowed moccasins.

"How did you know my name?" David demanded.

Fire Brush shrugged and kept walking. "Who doesn't know the famous David Blake, 'the Educated Injun'?" he said with a trace of a sneer. "I came here to help Stone Eagle, but he wandered off and I lost him."

"You know Stone Eagle?" David asked. He had to shuffle to keep the moccasins from sliding off his feet.

"Where would he go with a two jars of whiskey to drink?"

"How would I know and why would I want to help you?" David asked.

Fire Brush stopped and looked directly into his face. "Because you're an Indian and a fellow Indian needs you," he said, carefully enunciating each word. "And because Stone Eagle's your father and if we don't find him before those cowboys do, they'll kill him." He abruptly turned and started striding again. "Now, where to, Educated Injun?" he said over his shoulder.

David rubbed a hand over his face. This was all too fast and he didn't know if he liked this Fire Brush . If Stone Eagle was thinking at all, he'd probably want a place with some cover not too far from town. But who knew what he was thinking? David had no interest in finding him. What more could he say to him now that he'd punched him in the face?

"There's a small streambed about a quarter-mile from here with a couple of big cottonwood trees arching over it. He might go there to get out of the sun."

"Well, lead on, my educated friend. Or has all that book larnin' fogged up your mind?"

"We'll head straight out to the east to avoid town. We can come up the streambed from there," David said, shuffling his feet in the dust, extremely uneasy about sneaking around town with this Indian.

They walked in silence for five minutes or so and then David asked, "So, why do you give me so much grief about being educated?"

Fire Brush smiled. "Because, *Nemo propheta in patria sua*. In case you haven't kept up in your Latin studies, that means, 'No man is a prophet in his homeland.'" All that education doesn't mean anything here."

"Yeah, I get that," David said, cocking his head. "You're an educated Indian too. Where'd you learn Latin?"

"St. Augustine's' School for Boys in Leavenworth, Kansas," Fire Brush said. "In six years there they did everything they could to drive the Indian right out of me. And I mean everything."

David smiled and nodded his head. "Kill the Indian and save the man?" he asked with a wry smile.

"The priests were a little more diplomatic about it publicly, but it's the same theory," Fire Brush said, the smile fading from his face. "They did what they wanted to do to us. A boy either survived to become a man or he didn't . . . ever."

Fire Brush laughed bitterly, his voice thick in the hot afternoon air. "You don't think I look like someone who can speak Latin. Not to mention Greek, Spanish and French. And a medical degree from Princeton, too. Ten years ago I looked like you. Winston Allen Smith, they called me when I went back to Minnesota, the new Charles Eastman. All suit–and–tied, looking like a good little white boy. Only I wasn't. I wasn't white. That was made clear to me. And I wasn't Indian, either. That was make clear as well."

They had cleared the buildings of the town and were crossing open prairie toward the dry creek bed. In the oversized moccasins, David struggled to keep up with the long-legged Indian man.

Fire Brush's voice took on a hard edge as he turned and jammed a finger into David's chest. "The whites will tell you what you want to hear but when it comes down to it, you are just a savage in a suit. Oh sure, they'll ease their conscience by getting you educated and making sure you can talk well, but when it comes right down to it, you'd better be ready to practice your trade back on the reservation where you belong. And do it like they tell you. No white man's going to trust himself or his money to an Indian, no matter how he's dressed. And no Indian's going to take a job away from a white man." He slapped David on the chest with a thump.

"In fact, since you're better educated than most of the ignorant whites in the country, they resent you even more. They have to express their insecurity through bigotry, like those cowboys in front of the store." Fire Brush ran a finger along the scar over his left eye brow. "They're only too happy to point out that educated Indians bleed just as well as uneducated ones. I don't know where I was treated worse, in school or out. Some of the scars you see and some you don't."

David nodded his head as they made their through the sagebrush. In the last two weeks he'd had similar thoughts.

"Since the white man rejects the educated Indian, you'd think the Indians would appreciate him." Fire Brush snorted. "They're worse. They figure that the education taints him from the Great Spirit or something. Can you imagine a Great Spirit that would reward ignorance and self-pity?"

"You don't have much respect for your fellow man, white or Indian," David said as he regarded this remarkable individual with growing admiration.

"Maybe you're right, oh Educated One."

David pointed to a clump of cottonwood trees overhanging the streambed they had been following. "That's the place. You should be careful not scare him off." He turned to walk back to town.

Fire Brush grabbed David by the arm and pulled him to the trees. "If he stole that whiskey three hours ago, we'll have nothing to worry about. He'll be dead to the world."

Three trees leaned over the creek bed, bent by years of wind, rain and snow. Their branches swept almost to the ground over the creek bed, creating a living cave with walls and roof of shimmering leaves. David and Evan had used the trees as a hiding place and fort in happier times.

The remains of a freshly broken jar on the rocks in the streambed confirmed David's guess as to where Stone Eagle might be.

Dreading what he might see, he pulled back one of the branches. Although the trees shaded the streambed, they also held in the air. It seemed stale and smelled of alcohol and sweat.

As his eyes adjusted to the filtered light, he heard loud snoring. A large lump of rags slumped against a dead log in the streambed. Looking closer, David could see the lump heaving gently with each breath.

Fire Brush pulled the branch further away. "This is what the white man has turned us into."

David didn't remember his father. In the darkness by the livery stable, he never even saw the man's face clearly before he punched it.

From the time he was very young he knew that the Blakes were not his real parents. He'd been told that he didn't have a mother and father and that the Blakes were his parents now.

That was until the other night at Warner's store. When Evan told him his father gave him to the Blakes, he briefly had an image of a noble warrior reluctantly turning over his child to be raised in a better environment. Then he rejected the scenario. He'd been around enough alcohol-ravaged Indians at the school to know what the real story probably was. The reservation had turned many a brave Lakota warrior into a stinking drunk.

Fire Brush pushed through the branches and shook Stone Eagle roughly. "Wake up, you drunken fool."

The lump of clothing turned over and groaned. David saw a bloated and bruised face through straggly black hair. Stone Eagle didn't open his eyes. Fire Brush roughly slapped him in the face, making the pudgy skin shake. "Wake up, I tell you. There's someone here to see you!" Fire Brush yelled into Stone Eagle's face, his nose only inches away.

His small eyes opened slowly and he blinked at the intense look on the face of Fire Brush. David saw a look of recognition come into his face. "Away from me," he grumbled and pushed him to the side. "Leave me alone."

Fire Brush grabbed Stone Eagle's chin. "Wake up, you drunken fool. You're in danger! Sit up and act like a man. I brought you Crow Eyes. Is this the way you want your son to see you?"

Stone Eagle's face registered shock. He made an effort to collect himself and looked up. Fire Brush pointed across the shaded streambed to David, who was still holding the branch away from him. "This is the son you left to be raised by the white killers."

The big man turned toward David and stared. Tear welled in his eyes. It looked like he was having trouble comprehending. His lips moved but no sound came out.

"Why did you bring me here . . . to . . . that?" David said looking down at the crumpled form. "It has nothing to do with me."

"Your father wanted to talk to you. He needs you. Help him."

"I don't have a father," David said quietly, and took a step back, letting the branch drop, walling him off from the scene. He turned and walked down the streambed, his head bowed.

Fire Brush rushed out of the trees into the blinding sunlight. "You're a coward, a disgrace to your father. And a disgrace to your people!" he shouted, almost spitting the words.

"I have no father and no people," David shouted back at him, his voice rising in the thick hot air. "Not Indian and not white. I'm not an eagle or a hawk! I'm just nothing, got it? Nothing!" He turned and shuffled down the streambed in his suit pants, wrinkled dirty white shirt and ill-fitting moccasins.

Chapter Fourteen

THE COOL OF THE SUMMER NIGHT wrapped pleasantly around Evan's face as he snuggled beneath the buffalo robe Morgan had thrown over him. The heat from his body flowed from beneath the robe to his throat and face.

In what seemed only minutes, Evan heard Morgan stirring up the fire a few feet away. He didn't open his eyes. Maybe he could just live in this luxurious state between sleeping and waking forever.

"Come on, boy," Morgan said, nudging him lightly with his boot. "Time to get back to town."

Evan opened his eyes. Stars still sparkled in the dark, early morning sky. After a day of working cattle, he and Morgan had stayed up talking far into the night again, watching the fire burn from flames to bright orange embers and then to dark black clouds. He wanted to stay out on the ranch with Morgan forever. Raising his head, he saw the old cowboy already had a healthy cooking fire going and was boiling water.

"Good thing about stayin' up all night is that there's warm coals to start a mornin' fire. Can't have you sleepin' all day, though. We gotta get into town."

A pale light grew in the blue-black sky. The morning star stood guard over the horizon.

"Won't be daylight for another hour, and by that time we can be a healthy chunk of the way to town." The old cowboy handed him a cup of steaming coffee. Evan had never drunk coffee before and he frowned as the bitter taste filled his mouth. Morgan laughed and said, "The second sip'll be better. If you're gonna be a man on the range you need to drink strong coffee."

Evan smiled and took a second sip, feeling the hot liquid spread through his chest and out to his limbs. It tasted a little better. "You want me to meet you and Blue in town?" he asked, blowing the steam off his cup and feeling the heat on his lips.

"Naw, I'm thinkin' that you and me and Blue will walk together around the outside," Morgan said. He smiled, his yellowed teeth just visible in the early morning light. "Safety in numbers, you know."

He was surprised because Morgan always rode Blue to town. The old rancher's company would make the hike go faster.

Morgan poured some cornmeal into what was left of the boiling water and told Evan to pack up. Reluctantly, Evan crawled out into the early morning air and stuffed his extra clothes and canteen into his bag. The air was crisp. It wouldn't be long until summer slipped off into fall.

After wolfing down a few bites of boiled cornmeal, he helped Morgan clean up around the fire. They hauled the cleaned pots to Morgan's soddy, where they slid them into their assigned shelves. He noticed how few and simple Morgan's cooking utensils were compared to his mother's cluttered shelves. The rancher's few cooking tools were all well-used and impeccably clean.

By the time the first rays of sun peeked over the horizon, they were more than two miles on their way into town. While there was no dew on the grass, the early morning air was moist.

Sometimes they chatted as they walked and then they would walk in silence for long periods. Somehow, the silence and conversation both seemed less forced and stressful than ever. Now Morgan talked to him more as a peer than a lesson-giver. When there was silence, Evan didn't feel the need to fill the air with questions. He hadn't felt this at ease since before David left for school.

The early morning sun caressed the hauntingly beautiful spires of the Badlands. They glowed in the yellow light, offset by the dark shadows of the crags still waiting to be kissed by the morning sun.

The Badlands looked completely different in the morning light than they did at midday or evening. Evan noticed that they also looked different to him based on the mood he was in—the same scenery could be harsh and difficult, or beautiful and inviting. He hadn't been to many places, but the Badlands were a world unto themselves. He felt no need to ever leave.

As the buildings of Interior came in sight, Evan was almost sorry the walk was over. The cool, moist air of the dawn was giving way to the hot, dusty heat of the day. A haze of dust was already wafting over the town.

"Well," Morgan said. "Let's see what kind of trouble everyone got into while we were gone." He sucked his teeth and chuckled quietly.

They headed for Warner's store first. Morgan halted in front to tie up old Blue and Evan opened the door for him. He hesitated before taking a deep breath and walking into the darkness of the store. His father looked up from the back counter, where he was stacking bolts of cloth. His eyes darted from Morgan to Evan. An uncomfortable silence hung in the air.

Evan felt a stirring deep in his stomach and he shifted his weight from one foot to the other nervously as the calm of the morning left him. His father looked at Evan and gave him a small smile. "I was wonderin' when you two were going to stop gallivanting around the Badlands and come back to town. We got work to do!"

Relief swept over Evan like a wave. He felt the tension leave his shoulders and he leaned against the post in the middle of the room. He opened his mouth to tell his father all about the last two nights, but held back. "I just needed a little time away, I guess," was all he said.

His father nodded his head and ran a hand over his thinning hair. "We missed you two this week. Morgan, I don't know if Evan told you that Stone Eagle was back in town." He kept his hands busy folding the bolts of cloth.

"Yeah," Morgan said in a slow, confident voice. "Sounds like Amanda Blake probably scared him to death." His body shook as he laughed silently and winked at Evan.

James watched the old cowboy and his son look at each other and pursed his lips as he sucked in air. He and Evan had not had many little side looks in a long time. "Well . . . things are a little more serious now." His voice had an ominous tone. "Someone broke into the store and took all my whiskey. Didn't touch nothin' else."

"Ah, jeez," Morgan said, quickly stifling his laughter. "Any sign of him around?"

"No," he said as he snapped a bolt of cloth to get the wrinkles out. "But it gets worse. Those two cowboys that had been haulin' pack horses and tryin' to guide for Lauper made a big stink about it yesterday and went lookin' for him. Seems they got fired by Lauper 'cause they'd rather hunt for an Indian than a sheep. Now they want to go after Stone Eagle for attacking the Blakes and stealin' whiskey."

Morgan shook his head and pushed his hat up high on his head. Evan noticed the dollar-sized scar from Wounded Knee on his forehead again, now that he knew where to look for it. "Just what we need is a buncha' no account cowboys bein' vigilantes. For all of our sakes, I hope they track drunken Indians as well as they track mountain sheep."

The door to the store flew open with a bang, causing them all to jump. Amanda Blake burst into the store looking uncharacteristically disheveled. Strands of hair hung in disarray from her bun and her dress looked like she'd slept in it. "Morgan," she said, clutching his arm. "I saw your horse outside. Is David with you by any chance? I haven't seen him since yesterday."

The old cowboy stared down at the thin white hands on the cuff of his wrinkled blue shirt and then looked into her wild eyes.

"Jeezus, Amanda, you about scared me death bangin' the door like that. Evan and me were out at the ranch last couple nights. Ain't seen David at all." He held his arm away from his body as she continued to grasp it.

"Evan," James said, "David stopped by the other morning after you . . . ummm . . . left. He said he'd talked to you. Did he say where he was going?"

Recalling the wrestling match in the dirt made Evan smile. It seemed like such a long time ago. "He didn't say where he was going. Did he stop here?"

"He, ahh . . . we talked," James said, a slight smile crossing his face. "Well, I guess mostly he talked." He turned to Amanda. "He's a good boy, Amanda, more of a man than a boy, really. I'm sure he'll be just fine."

"Oh, James, I don't know. He was so angry when he left yesterday afternoon." She was still gripping Morgan's arm. "Why, he took off his shoes and threw them down the road. What would possess a boy to throw away a perfectly good pair of shoes?" When she shook her head, strands of her hair flowed back and forth like they were in the wind.

Evan had seen Mrs. Blake every day at school since he was a first-year student, and she always was very neatly groomed. It was unsettling to see her so rumpled and agitated.

They heard several horses approach and voices outside the store. "Oh, God, it's time for the parade," James said from behind the counter. "I wonder who they'll have with them this time."

Morgan looked confused. He forced the arm Amanda Blake was still gripping away from his body, and she finally released it. "What parade?" he growled.

Evan smiled and clapped Morgan on the back. "Every day when the Lauper group heads out to hunt the ram they parade through town at the same time—nine o'clock on the dot," he said.

"They leave town to hunt at nine in the morning?" Morgan said with scorn. "No wonder they can't find anything." He walked toward the open door, followed closely by Mrs. Blake.

"Oh no!" she said from the porch in front of the store, raising a hand to her mouth. "He can't!"

When Evan got to the door he saw over Mrs. Blake's shoulder what had upset her. The Lauper hunting party was led as usual by Colonel Lauper and next to him on his fifteen-hand horse was Rafe Colton, looked as confident and flashy as ever. As they pulled even with the store he saw a second file of riders including Lauper's assistant, Windsor, and a familiar figure in dark pants and white shirt. It was David, riding a gray mare.

He rode with his head low, an old straw hat pulled over his eyes. His dark suit pants and white shirt were wrinkled and dirty. On his feet were leather moccasins, from which his bare heels swung free.

"David!" Mrs. Blake shouted, cupping her hand to her mouth. She took a quick step across the boardwalk toward the riders.

James reached out and gently grasped her shoulder, holding her on the wooden walkway. "Amanda, don't," he said as he pulled her back toward the store. "He knows you're here. Don't make it worse."

David rode with his eyes to the ground. The group in front of the store watched the riders amble toward the Badlands. All was silent except for the uneven sounds of the horses' gaits.

Amanda groaned and turned toward James, her body slumped in dismay. "What's he doing?" she asked in a desperate voice. "I told him explicitly, I didn't want him out there chasing that damned sheep."

Morgan sucked his teeth and responded, "I suspect he's doing 'explicitly' what you told him not to do, ma'am. It's all part of growin' up." He sighed and pulled his hat back over his forehead, covering his scar.

"He'll be fine, Amanda," James said with a side glance at Morgan. "He's a good boy, and almost a man. There are some decisions he needs to make for himself. Standing in his way won't help him and it certainly won't help you." He led her into the store as gently as he could. "Why don't you have a cup of coffee with us? Where's Edmund?"

"Oh, he's at home doing nothing. Nobody's doing anything to help." She fretted at the straggly hair in her eyes, as if only now realizing her unkempt state. "That man's good for nothing."

"Amanda . . ." James began, reaching out to touch her shoulder.

"Oh, what will everyone say?" She spun out of his grasp and stormed out the door. She hesitated for a moment at the street, sighed, then started for home with quick, angry steps.

Deloris entered from the back door and asked, "Did I miss the parade? Where's Amanda off to?"

Her bright, dark eyes suddenly fell on Evan and she rushed over and hugged him. "I'm so glad you're back," she whispered in his ear. "I don't know what you see out in that godforsaken place."

"Well, it isn't so bad," Morgan rumbled. "The way you talk about the Badlands, it sounds like Hell itself." He was standing in the middle of the room leaning against a support post.

Deloris relaxed her grip on her son and gave Morgan's arm a squeeze. "All the same, I'm glad you're back," she said with a glance to Morgan. "Both of you." The old cowboy didn't move. He wasn't used to women squeezing his arm all the time and didn't look like he cared much for it.

"Well," Evan said, sliding out of his mother's hug and trying to change the subject. "I guess that Lauper guy's going to be famous, then. If anybody can track the ram down, it's David."

James watched his son for several seconds and then walked behind the back counter. He reached into the shelf and pulled out the old hunting rifle. It had been cleaned and smelled of gun oil. He put a box of shells on the counter beside the rifle and said, "Evan, it's all yours. If you want to hunt that sheep, go to it."

His eyes lit up. "You mean it, Pa? Are we going to put it on display here?"

"If you shoot the sheep, you do what you want with it. You're the hunter. It's your responsibility." He stepped back against the wall. "Evan," his voice dropped to barely above a whisper. "I umm . . . I'm sorry. David told me you overheard us arguing." He looked up to meet Deloris's eyes and smiled, shaking his head with what looked like embarrassment. "In fact he gave me quite a talking to. I don't think you're stupid. I just . . ."

It was Evan's turn to look surprised. "It's okay, Pa," he said as he ran his hand along the barrel of the rifle. He paused and, with a look over toward Morgan, said, "You know, it probably isn't okay, but we all make mistakes. Just don't make excuses, Pa. We'll just go on. I'm going to try not to make excuses from now on myself." He turned toward his mother. "What's for breakfast?"

She laughed and gave Evan another quick hug. "Somehow I knew that was the next thing on your mind. You all just wait right here. I'll bring in some breakfast and we can all eat together." She raised her chin and attempted to imitated the Windsor's English accent, "I'm not cehtain if its lunch or breakfast, but we'll enjoy presently."

She slid out from under Evan's arm and glided out the back of the store to the house. Evan thought even he saw her skip once on the way.

He watched his mom and then looked at the two men. James had returned to stacking the cloth behind the counter and seemed to be avoiding his gaze. Morgan still leaned against the post, studying his watch. Most of the energy in the room had left with his mother.

"So you goin' out after that ol' ram, then?" Morgan asked.

"Yeah, I'm going to find it before that Lauper guy gets a shot at him." Evan said, bouncing on the balls of his feet and running his fingers over the stock of the rifle. "Do you want to come with me?"

Morgan was slow to answer as he scratched his back against the support post like an old bear. "No, I figure I'll leave the trophies to you all."

There was an uncomfortable silence as Evan continued to run his fingers over the rifle and looked from Morgan to his father. Neither of them seemed particularly excited about the fact that he was going to hunt the ram.

"Ummm, I'm going to help Mom with breakfast," he said setting the rifle carefully on counter. "I'll help her carry things out." Morgan nodded and his father continued to busy himself behind the counter. Evan had a feeling that they were going to have a discussion as soon as he left the room.

He pushed open the back door and walked through the lean-to into the little house. His mom was humming to herself in the kitchen as she fried thick bacon in a cast iron skillet.

She looked up and smiled, a small sheen of sweat on her forehead from the heat of the stove. The smell of bacon filled the kitchen and made his stomach growl.

"I'm so proud of your father. You know it wasn't easy for him to admit he was wrong and get that gun fixed for you."

"Yeah, I know. Now." He slid into a chair at the table. "Why does he treat me like a kid so often?" He picked up a piece of warm bread that she had just cut.

She reached over, took the bread out of his hands and moved the loaf out of his reach. "Wait for the meal," she said sternly. "Evan, a few years may seem like a long time to you, but it wasn't that long ago you were just a baby. You depended on your father and me for everything."

She returned to frying the bacon. "Growing up is hard. It's hard on all of us. It won't be long before you're all grown up and will be responsible for yourself. You won't need us," She drained the grease from the bacon into a stone jar and set the bacon on a plate. Then she poured a bowl full of beaten eggs into the skillet. "Your father was just trying to protect you." She speared one slice of bacon with a fork and held it out to him. He avoided the fork and greedily grabbed the bacon, burning the tips of his fingers. "Evan, for goodness' sake, that's hot!" she said with exasperation.

Ignoring her admonition he asked, "Why did he decide to let me hunt the ram? Did you talk him into it?"

"I did and David did. Evidently your father and David had quite a conversation," she said as she scrambled the eggs. "James said he's really grown up."

"He didn't look too grown up today riding out with Lauper," Evan countered. He pushed the rest of the bacon into his mouth. "He wouldn't even look up at us," he said through a mouthful of crispy meat.

"I'm sure he's having a tough time. Just going to all those teas with Amanda would about drive a person crazy," she said with an amused smile. Then her face colored a deep shade of pink, "And don't you say that to anyone," she said scrambling the eggs with more energy than was necessary. "Your father's trying his best and you need to help." Evan couldn't think of what he should say and only smiled.

"Now get the plates and take them into the store, she said. "If there are customers in there, they'll just have to watch us eat."

THE FOUR OF THEM were just finishing the last of their meal when they heard quick footsteps on the wooden walkway.

The front door opened again with a bang. "Jeezus," Morgan exclaimed as he jumped and almost spilled his coffee. "Don't nobody ever walk through that door normal-like anymore?"

Terrel rushed into the room trailed by a dark-skinned man who looked like an Indian. The reporter looked utterly frazzled. "They found him! Those cowboys have that Indian," he gasped between breaths.

"Ahhh, hell," Morgan said, moving with surprising quickness to the wall by the front door where he had left his bag. He pulled out his old .45 pistol. "Where are they?"

"The big cottonwood on the south side of town," the Indian man said. "Stone Eagle was passed out when they found him."

Morgan squinted and looked at the man from head to toe. "Who are you?"

"My name's Fire Brush," he said. "I've been traveling with Stone Eagle. A couple of days ago, I left him for just a few minutes to get some food, and when I came back, he was gone. Now they found him. I don't have a gun, and there was nothing I could do." Terrel wiped the sweat off his forehead. "They said they're gonna hang him."

"Damned fools," Morgan muttered. He stomped across the room and out the door, his boots striking hard on the wooden walkway in front of the store.

Evan grabbed the rifle where it lay on the counter and fumbled to open the box of shells. He grabbed a handful, jammed them in his pocket and followed Morgan.

"Evan," his father called. "You . . ."

On his way out, Evan looked back for an instant at his parents. Then he continued out the door, jamming a shell into the gun as he walked.

Morgan was striding purposefully down the middle of the street, the .45 swinging loosely in his right hand. Evan jogged a little to catch up and fell into step beside him.

Morgan glanced over at him. He gave him a half-smile and then turned serious again. "Don't you point that at a man unless you're ready to kill him," he said with grim intent.

"Yessir," was all that Evan could think of to say. If Morgan had told him to go back, he figured he probably would. It didn't seem real that he could be walking down the middle of the road with Morgan, both of them carrying loaded guns.

They rounded the corner at the end of the main street and saw two horses tied up under the large spreading branches of the cotton-wood tree. From fifty yards away, they could make out two men. One was standing over a prone body and the other was holding a rope.

The short, pudgy cowboy was trying to throw the rope over a large branch of the tree and was not having much luck. Each time he missed both of the men would laugh at each other hysterically. A half-full jar at the base of the tree indicated that Stone Eagle had not drunk all of the whiskey taken from Warner's store. The way the two cowboys were staggering around and laughing, it was clear that they had been sampling the evidence.

"What is it that you boys are tryin' to do?" Morgan asked, limping toward them and nudging Evan to the right. "Twenty feet," he said under his breath.

The two cowboys turned to face them, surprised at being interrupted. "We're fixin' to hang this buck for whiskey stealin' and white woman attackin'," the smaller cowboy said, sounding as if no one could object to their action.

"'Cept ol' Bob here can't throw a rope." The larger cowboy with the black beard was laughing so hard he nearly stumbled over the slumped body on the ground.

"Shut up, Drager," Bob said, frowning. "Ain't seen you do no better."

Morgan took two steps closer and stopped, nodding at Evan to do the same. "I think you two should just move on." His voice was so calm and commanding that the men stopped laughing. "Fun's over. We'll take care of the Indian."

"I told you, old man," Drager said scornfully. "This here Indian attacked a white woman and stole whiskey. And he's probably the one that's wanted, too." He kicked dust at the figure lying on the ground with his hands tied. Stone Eagle's moved slightly but didn't struggle.

Then Morgan spoke in a more forceful voice. "Ain't nobody been attacked and looks to me that you been into that whiskey as much as he has. It's time for you to all just move on outta this part of the country." He nodded at the horses standing on the other side of the tree.

Drager laughed, his teeth bright white against his black beard. "I suppose an old man and a boy are gonna stop us." He stuck his chin out and sneered.

Evan heard footsteps on the road. He glanced back to see his father and Fire Brush walking up behind them. James was holding a shotgun. Fifty steps back he could see Terrel's head poking out from behind the last house on the main street.

"Oh, a shopkeeper and store Injun too now, I see." Drager laughed. "You all just watch how a hangin' should be done." He grabbed the rope from Bob and awkwardly threw it back toward the branch. The loop hung on top for an instant and then collapsed back to the ground.

Morgan took two slow steps toward Drager. "It looks to me like we got four determined men here who ain't gonna let you hang that Indian. Over there you got two drunk cowboys who got nothin' better to do with themselves." He took another step closer. "This ain't somethin' worth getting killed over, cowboy." Morgan still held the .45 loosely in his right hand at his side. With his other hand, he fished his watch out of his pocket, never taking his eyes off the cowboys.

Bob backed a step away from Drager and Stone Eagle. "Come on, Drager. Let's let these yokels have their damned Indian."

Morgan glanced down at his watch like he had somewhere else to go.

Evan felt the tension starting to flow away. Bob slowly walked to where the horses were tied and took the reins.

"Ah, hell, you're probably right," Drager said, leaning over to pick up the half-full bottle. "It is just a drunk Injun. I don't know what everybody is so excited about."

"Take it," Morgan said sharply, snapping his watch shut and taking another step closer to the men. "An' leave town."

Drager straightened up and pointed to James and then Stone Eagle. "Shopkeeper, ain't there a reward for finding this here thief?"

"You're gettin' outta here without gettin' shot, aren't you," James Warner said. His voice was harder than Evan had ever heard it. "Take the rest of the bottle and don't come back."

Drager faced the men, his feet spread. "I figure I'll go wherever I want." He let his free hand drift toward his holstered gun. His eyes met Morgan's. Swearing under his breath, he turned and climbed up on his mount. He pulled his hat down low over his eyes. "Ain't nothing in this damned town worth stayin' for anyway. You can have your damned Indian," he said as he roughly turned his horse and slowly ambled to the north. After one sullen look at the four men, Bob followed him.

Morgan walked over to where Stone Eagle was lying. He kneeled beside him and worked on untying the knots holding his wrists behind his back. The big Indian didn't move. Small pebbles were stuck to his cheek and his eyes were glassy.

"I'm not sure he even knows what just happened," James said looking down with disapproval at Stone Eagle.

"What's wrong with him?" Evan asked as he moved over to stand next to his father.

Fire Brush knelt down on the other side of Stone Eagle. "Combination of shock and booze, I suspect," he said, helping Morgan free Stone Eagle's arms. "He'll come around in a day or so." He looked up at the men. "I've done everything I could for him. I . . . I didn't know what to do about those guys."

"Them drunk cowboys warn't gonna do nothin' in front of white men," Morgan said. "It was a good thing you came and got us."

Terrel arrived after running the last fifty feet in the hot sun. He was breathing hard and his face was covered with sweat. "That was amazing! Most exciting thing I've seen in years! An old man, a shopkeeper, an unarmed Indian and a boy, standing down two desperados to save the life of a noble Indian warrior!" he gushed. Evan rolled his eyes.

Morgan looked over his shoulder at Terrel. But before he could say anything James spoke. "It was four men standing up to two drunken bullies. If you print anything more than that I'll call you a liar all across the state."

Terrel looked confused. "This is a story that needs to be told. Why, it could be a dime novel in itself. Worth hundreds of dollars. Could bring people in from—"

"You try to tell it and I'll tell everyone how you couldn't see any of it because you were hiding behind that house," James said with a smile.

"If'n you'll excuse me," Morgan drawled. "I think I'll take this 'noble Indian warrior' back to the ranch with me and see if we can't get him sobered up." He looked over at Fire Brush, "'Less you want to take him?"

Fire Brush shook his head. "I've done everything I can for him. I think I've had enough of the West. Out here, I can't be white and I can't be Indian. I'm going back East and resume my life as a white Indian."

He helped Morgan pull Stone Eagle to his feet and they each supported an arm. The big man's feet dragged awkwardly as he stumbled back toward town between the two men.

"It's probably a good idea to get both of you out of town," James said to Fire Brush. "If those cowboys come back, they'll be looking for any Indian they can find."

Morgan shook his head. "I don't think they'll be back," he said, "but you're probably right. I'll take Stone Eagle out to the ranch." He looked over at Fire Brush. "You can come too, if you want."

Fire Brush shook his head. "I already told you. I've had enough of the West. I'm going to the nearest train."

James looked over at Morgan. "You can use our horse to take him to the ranch, if you like." He hesitated, "Unless you want to take the horse hunting, Evan."

That surprised Evan. His father had never allowed him to take the horse anywhere except when he was running errands for the store. "That's okay," he said. "In the Badlands a horse just slows you down. Besides, I'm not going out until tomorrow, anyway. I was going to help you get the store restocked."

His father put an arm around Evan's shoulders and they walked back toward town with Morgan, Fire Brush and the staggering Stone Eagle. Terrel stood beneath the tree, furiously scribbling in his notebook.

Chapter Fifteen

DAVID'S EYES NEVER LEFT the dusty mane of the skinny sorrel they gave him to ride. He felt the town around him. Peripherally, Warner's store came into view and then the figure of Mrs. Blake in the doorway. He heard her voice but didn't register what she was saying. He wasn't sure what he would do if she confronted him. He wasn't sure if he wanted her to. He just wasn't sure of anything.

The last few hours had been a blur. The revulsion he felt at seeing his father, his own flesh and blood, lying there in a drunken heap rattled him to his core. The other Indian man, Fire Brush's taunts hovered in his thoughts. The drunken man passed out on the ground had nothing to do with him. His people! He had no people. Not the Lakota who had abandoned him, not the whites who tried to mold him, not anybody. He was his own person, only he wasn't sure if that was true either. He wasn't anything.

Once they left town the noise stopped, anyway. He thought he might have seen Evan and Morgan out of the corner of his eye in front of the store. He didn't owe them anything. They didn't understand. They weren't so pure. They just didn't understand

"Hey, Indian Kid," Colton's voice rang through the morning air. "Where are we goin'? You're supposed to be the guide, get to guidin'."

David looked up from beneath the old straw hat someone, maybe Windsor, had shoved on his head this morning. They were approaching the first spires of the Badlands, white-gray against the perfectly blue sky. He had not been inside the Badlands in over two years, since he and Evan had explored them. Where would the old ram be? Someplace remote would probably be best. "Ummm, around to the west, there's a gap that will get us to the plateaus," he said.

Colton shaded his eyes and looked at the rough broken country to the west. "We been working the ravines around the east and north," he said.

"Yeah, and you haven't seen any sign." David felt some of his old confidence coming back. The fog that had enveloped him in town was starting to clear and the rough broken prairie of the Badlands came into closer focus. "It will take us a few hours and we'll have to lead the horses some, but those inside plateaus are remote and a good place for him to hide." He really didn't know anything about Audubon Sheep, but if he was going to hide away from men, that's where he would go.

Colton let loose a long string of spit and shoved his wad of tobacco deeper into his cheek. "By the time we work our way through those breaks we won't have no time for huntin'," he said looking over at Colonial Lauper.

"Then maybe we should have left before nine in the morning," David said, turning his horse to the west. He didn't care if they chose to follow him or not. At this point he really didn't care if he got fired. He only took the job to . . . Why did he take this job? He still wasn't sure.

The grumbling the background told him that Colton and the rest of the party was following. Without looking back he led them through the rough breaks that separated the Badlands from the open prairie to the south. He halted and climbed down from the gray mare. "We'll have to lead the horses from here. We'll follow this ravine up to that gap and then down the other side to the middle fields," he said pointing to a low spot between two spires."

"We will stop here for lunch and to evaluate," Colonial Lauper said as he scanned the ravine. "Windsor, please get our meal prepared."

They led the horses to where the bank had been cut away, casting a shadow across the ravine. David took his sandwich and walked down to another shady spot at the next bend. The roast beef was tender and the bread was soft and white against his fingers. He leaned his head back against the bank and closed his eyes to let the heat of the Badlands flow over him.

"You seem to be recovering," a voice said.

The English-accented voice seemed out of place in the Badlands. It took awhile for David to even register that it was Windsor who had spoken to him. The little Englishman lowered himself to sit next to him. When he spoke again David almost expected the words to come out in a western accent, but sure enough it was formal King's English floating across the Badlands ravine. "I said, Master Blake, that you appear to be recovering rather nicely. In camp this morning you were quite distracted."

"Yes," David said. "The situation in town was . . . difficult. Out here . . ." he swept his arm across the spires. "Out here, it is simpler."

"Agreed," the little Englishman said. "There is a feeling here like no other place I've ever been. It is both freeing and exhilarating."

David was surprised to hear that Windsor enjoyed the Badlands. The harsh, dry country was the exact opposite of what he thought the Englishman would like. "I'm glad you like it," he replied. Pointing over to where Colton was unleashing another stream of profanity at the Badlands spires and the climb in front of them, he said, "It doesn't appear that Mr. Colton has quite the same view."

Windsor smiled. Colton had whined and complained every time the party passed the first of the gray-white mounds surrounding the Badlands. "I believe the Bad Lands, as you call them, have a way of stripping away the façades men tend to build around themselves. With the false images removed, the only thing left is the real essence of the man. Mr. Colton over there has spent so much time and energy creating his desired persona, there isn't much left to confront the reality of this place."

David looked at the little Englishman in astonishment. He hadn't spoken more than a few curt words to him and now he was philosophizing about the country where David felt strongest. And he was right. When the party entered the Badlands the responsibilities of education and class had melted away. Beneath the high spires, the tea parties and prejudices and family and race responsibilities flowed away into the deep ravines. With every step into the harsh country the clouds surrounding his head in town had cleared.

Windsor continued. "That is why your friend Evan Warner thrives so out here. As he is without pretension, the energy of the Badlands is free to fill him. Completely the opposite of poor Mr. Colton, I'm afraid." He turned to smile at David. "We can all learn something from young master Warner."

David found his point a little insulting. He pictured himself dressed in his new suit, smiling and shaking hands in Warner's store. The image of the puppet show presented at his school flashed across his mind. "What about you? Don't you find all of your 'English butler' image difficult to maintain out here?"

The small man raised one corner of his mouth in a half-smile and shook his head. He rose and dusted of his pants, carefully picking a small burr off his thigh. He started to walk away and then paused, saying, "An 'English butler' is exactly what I am." He turned back to look at David. "And that is why I can appreciate the Badlands." He walked back toward where the rest of the party was gathering their things to return to the hunt.

"Come on, Indian Kid," Colton bellowed, his voice filling the ravine. "The sooner we find that damned sheep the sooner we can get the hell out of here."

David rose and dusted off his pants. It was going to be a long afternoon.

Chapter Sixteen

THE SUN HAD REACHED a high point in the sky, baking the Badlands. The harsh glare off the clay eliminated every shadow and parched the ground into a cracking crust.

Evan pulled his hat down low over his eyes. Since midmorning he had been concentrating on hunting the deep ravines, partly because he thought he might see a track somewhere and partly because it provided some relief from the brutal sun.

So far, he'd seen no sign of the ram. The hard clay that filled the bottom of the ravines was too dry to hold a track for very long. Morgan had taught him to look deep into the bends of the oxbows for shaded places where some moisture had accumulated and the ground was softer.

Yesterday he'd watched Morgan and Stone Eagle quietly ride out of town toward the ranch. Terrel had been uncharacteristically quiet about the incident by the cottonwood tree. Apparently, his father's threat to tell everyone that Terrel was cowering behind the little house while the drama was unfolding had the desired effect. At dinner, his father said that Terrel would probably go ahead and write whatever he wanted to, but not until after he left Interior. Somehow, Evan felt better about that. He really didn't care what was said outside of town.

He'd spent the day in the store helping his father. When Colton and some of the other hunters came in that night, no mention was made of the incident by the cottonwood. When Colton asked if the Indian who stole the whiskey had been found, his father just shrugged his shoulders. Evan was as proud of his father for the shrug as he was for his actions at the cottonwood tree.

"Well, that Indian kid we hired sure knows his way around the Badlands," Colton had said. "According to him, those other idiots had been looking in all the wrong spots. Dunno if he'll find the sheep, but at least Lauper likes him."

Evan had listened eagerly to see if he could get more information about the hunt, but Colton changed the subject to talk about one of his exploits in Texas. He always pronounced it "Teejass, the way the Mexies do." Even though Terrel had pointed out to him that the "j" in *Tejas* in Spanish sounded like an "H," Colton ignored him with a glare and continued his story.

Evan had watched for David, eager to tell him about the rescue of Stone Eagle, but he hadn't come into town with the hunting party. When he asked Colton where he was, the showman said, "The boy vanished right after we came out of the Badlands. That crazy Blake woman was waitin' for him at the camp, mad as hell when he wasn't with us. I just told her to vacate the premises."

Evan's mother had gotten up to fix him breakfast before first light and his father had been almost too helpful in getting everything together, as if he were trying to make up for lost time. Evan had wanted to tell him, "I'm just going huntin', not on a week-long trip," but he enjoyed having their support after so much complaining about his previous Badlands adventures. He wondered what David had said to his father to to inspire such a marked change in his attitude toward Evan.

By midday, he'd been working the Badlands ravines for hours and hadn't seen any sign of the ram. After the send-off from his parents, he felt guilty and incompetent. What if he hunted all day and returned without spotting a single sign?

For the first time since he left town, he heard human voices drifting up the dry wash. He leaned back against the slight overhang to get as much shade as he could and waited while the voices came closer.

Colton's rumbling voice was unmistakable. He was leading the way up the ravine on his great horse and David followed about ten feet back, leaning over his saddle looking for tracks along the side. When Colton saw Evan standing beneath the overhang, he spurred the big horse forward.

"You seen anything, Warner Kid?" he asked gruffly as he peered out from under his big floppy hat.

Evan shook his head.

"Our Indian Kid ain't found nothin' either. Nothin' for two days now. I don't think there is any damn sheep out here. You and that old coot musta just made the whole thing up," he said, wiping a gob of spit off his mustache with the back of his hand.

Evan just looked at the man and kicked at the sand at the bottom of the ravine. He didn't feel the least bit compelled to talk to the obnoxious blowhard. He watched as David walked his horse back from up the draw. "Hey, Indian Kid, you find anything this time?" Colton yelled.

David's eyes met Evan's, and then he looked over at Colton. "No, nothing up that draw. Let's try around the other side of Mystic Mountain. I think that's a much better place."

"Christ, now I gotta tell those Englishmen we've gotta ride for another hour. Let's just take them up this here draw anyway," He pointed to the saddle up the draw a half-mile away.

"Sure, if you want, but it'd be a complete waste of time. No sign a sheep's been up this draw in forever," David said, shaking his head.

Colton swore and turned his big horse back down the main wash. David reached out and grabbed Evan's arm. Under his breath with his lips barely moving he said, "Left bank, just past the overhang."

Shocked that David had spoken directly to him, Evan said, "What?" too loudly. Then, under his breath, "I can't hear you."

David gave him an exasperated look, his dark eyes flashing. "Damn it, Evan," he said in a pronounced whisper, "look on the left bank past the overhang." When Evan still looked perplexed, David said, "I don't want him to know," without moving his lips as he jerked his head toward Colton who was ambling on ahead on his big horse.

"What are you girls gabbing about?" Colton asked, turning back around. "You picking daisies? Warner Kid, you want to come with us to the other side of Mystic Mountain? You girls can chat while we ride. Maybe you and Indian Kid together could find that damned sheep."

"Ummm, no, sir . . . I . . . have to . . . ummmm, I'm going to look around here," he stammered, and David lightly kicked him. "But not in this draw. No . . . nothing here in this draw . . . but some other one. I . . ."

"Evan said he wants to try some of the lower valleys—more feed there," David said, walking his horse toward Colton. Then, turning to Evan, he said, "Good luck to you, and we'll see you tonight."

"Yeah, yeah, I . . ." Evan said quickly, nodding his head. "Gonna look in the lower valleys . . . not this draw."

David mounted and as the two riders continued down the wash, Evan heard Colton say, "I don't know about that Warner Kid. He says the dumbest things. Still, he sure seemed funny about that draw. I wonder if he saw something?"

"Is it true that Buffalo Bill Cody is the world's best wilderness scout, like the newspapers say?" David asked in a loud voice.

"Bill Cody, paaaaa." Colton glared at him and waved his hand over his head. "He couldn't find a buffalo if it was hidin' behind a pimple on his butt. Why, those newspapers spend all their time glorifying that blowhard sumbitch and he ain't never . . ."

Evan smiled as the two of them rode out of earshot. He quickly made his way over the left bank of the wash where David had been. He could easily follow his tracks in the soft clay at the wash bottom. Just past the overhang in the soft sand he spotted three clearly-defined sheep tracks. They were so fresh the sand was still damp in the bottom of the impressions.

He felt a huge surge of excitement. This was his chance! His stomach churned and he felt sweat break out all over his body.

With a quick look over his shoulder, he hurried up the smooth sand at the bottom of the ravine, watching for other tracks.

He almost broke into a run after he checked in the soft moist sand at the end of the next bend and found another fresh track. It appeared that the ram was walking up the ravine on the far right side in the shade of the overhang, leaving tracks in the moist sand at the end of the bends.

His heart racing, Evan decided to sit back and collect himself. "Make sure everything is ready before you need to shoot," he said to himself. He opened his bag for a rag and oil. Sitting in a sliver of shade at the edge of the streambed, he quickly cleaned the old Winchester and checked his shells. He knew he'd be lucky to get one shot, much less have time to reload, but he wanted to be ready.

Looking up at the sun, he saw that he had a good five or six hours of daylight. There was plenty of time to walk up the draw cautiously, so he wouldn't spook the ram.

The dry streambed narrowed as he gained elevation until it was just wide enough to walk in. As he rounded a ridgeline, he got his first glimpse of the top of the saddle between the two spires making up the ravine and the small bowl between them. "If he's here, he'll be back in that bowl," he mumbled to himself.

He scanned the ridges on either side of the ravine and chose the one to the left. It was topped by a series of boulders that would give him some cover. It would also put his back to the setting sun so it wouldn't be shining in his eyes. Unfortunately, climbing the bank up that side was going to be a steeper route.

He retreated down the dry streambed to where the climb looked a little easier and he'd be less likely to spook the ram. He slung the rifle on his back so he could use both hands to climb the bank.

It took more than half an hour of tedious scrambling to ascend the steep bank. He worked at an angle through the ankle-deep skree, grasping at any vegetation that attempted to grow on the steep slope. Toward the top of the incline the loose skree gave way to harder rock, which was easier to climb but was even steeper and more challenging.

As he looked back down he could see it would be a long drop if he slipped and slid down the slope. He unconsciously leaned into the bank. With the weight off his toes, they immediately slipped and he started to slide off the ledge.

He straightened up and dug his toes into the hard clay, feeling them grip. Pulling with his hands and kicking his feet as deeply into the clay as he could, he slowly pulled himself over the ledge.

He lay at the top of the ledge behind a large boulder, breathing hard. Thirty feet above him, the top of the ridge was considerably more open. He could stay on the ledge and be protected by the line of boulders. Sweat dripped from his face onto the dry clay of the Badlands. His fingers and palms were scraped and dirty and his legs ached, but he had made it.

Once his breathing finally returned to normal, he checked the rifle again. It had made it through the climb without filling with dirt.

He leaned out stealthily to peer around one of the boulders. He couldn't see the bowl from where he was. He crept slowly along the ledge, from boulder to boulder, getting closer to the bowl and being careful not to kick skree noisily down the slope.

Although his breathing had returned to normal, his heart was pounding. After all this time, he was going to see the ram again, and now he had a rifle.

He began to daydream about how excited everyone would be when he brought the trophy to town. He thought about posing for the photographer that Terrel had said he'd send for and how he'd tell his story. For some reason, he imagined Emily Johnson's smiling face in the front row. He could almost hear the applause and feel the pats on his back.

The ridge turned sharply and he could tell by the tops of the spires that he would soon be able to see the bowl. He reduced his pace even further, keeping his head down and moving as quietly as possible. The ledge line lay below the saddle of the spire so he knew he would not be silhouetted against the sky.

He settled in behind a large boulder where he could just around at the bowl.

Two spires framed the bowl, which had steep banks around three sides and, on the fourth, a shelf that dropped down into the deep ravine. The bottom of the bowl was almost perfectly flat and it had a light covering of green grass. Beyond the grassy level, Evan could see the blackness of a dark crack that was the head of the ravine.

It was such a stunning sight that he almost didn't notice the ram standing exactly in the middle of the grass, back far enough that it wouldn't be visible from the ravine below. Evan realized that Lauper himself could've ridden up to the very edge of that cliff, looked around, and not known that the ram was mere yards above him. The sun, high overhead, glinted off the massive spiral horns as the great animal lowered his head to graze on the young shoots of grass.

Enthralled, Evan could only observe the magnificent head bobbing up and down as the ram grazed peacefully, just as he had in this wilderness for uncounted years.

Evan slid back behind the boulder and unslung the rifle. Carefully loading the cartridge, he winced as the well-oiled bolt made a sharp click. He sat with his back to the boulder and raised his eyes to the sky. Sweat ran down the sides of his face in small droplets. He closed his eyes and took a deep breath. He pictured clearly in his mind exactly what he was going to do.

He slowly turned and slid along the rough surface of the boulder, keeping his head low. Peering around the edge, he almost hoped that the ram would be gone. In that split second, he could already imagine telling the story of how he found the ram but it ran off before he could get a shot off: the one that got away!

His stomach churned as he raised his head and saw that the ram had not moved. It continued to graze, oblivious to any threat.

He rested the old rifle on a spot he'd already picked out on the boulder. It was a perfect shot, seventy-five yards at the most. No wind. He sighted along the barrel and put a bead right on the ram's heart and lungs. It would be a clean shot. He couldn't bear to kill the ram with anything less than a perfectly clean shot. He almost hoped it would move so he'd have an excuse not to shoot.

The ram stopped grazing and looked up as if he'd heard something. The great golden eyes scanned the Badlands looking for a predator. Evan thought, *He hasn't seen me. I'm the one who is finally going to kill him.*

His finger found the smooth metal on the trigger. All he needed to do was to hold his breath and gently squeeze. The ram was sighted perfectly down the barrel. The clean smell of gun oil filled his nose. He drew a breath, tightened his stomach and willed his finger to squeeze the trigger.

But his finger wouldn't respond. His body began to shake. He felt tears welling up in his eyes. The vision of the ram blurred as his eyes filled. Long, painful seconds elapsed while Evan held his position, trembling, aching, unable to act, but unwilling to surrender.

Someone would shoot the sheep, but it wouldn't be him. He sighed as he rested his head on the stock of the old rifle and felt the hard smooth wood against his cheek. He raised his head saw the splash of a tear on the rifle butt.

He looked out at the ram one more time and it seemed as if he was looking at it eye-to-eye. The ram stood perfectly still, as if painted into a picture.

Evan turned and slid down the boulder to the ground. He had a feeling of relief tinged with regret. He wasn't sure if his feeling of relief and regret was for himself or the ram.

A loud crack shattered the quiet of the Badlands. He jumped and his rifle clattered to the ground. He swiftly poked his head back over the top of the boulder.

The great ram lay motionless on the green grass, the mighty head with its massive horns at rest on the ground. It was a clean shot. The last of the Audubon Sheep was dead.

Evan stood, thunderstruck, staring at the scene below him, his mouth agape. With a sinking feeling in his stomach he wondered where the shot had come from. Who had successfully bagged this trophy?

He heard a shuffling sound from behind him. Thirty feet up on the top of the saddle, he could see a man's figure silhouetted against the sky. There was no mistaking the figure of the lanky old rancher.

"My god, Morgan!" Evan shouted, his voice shaking and his eyes filled with tears. "What've you done?"

Morgan looked down at him from beneath the brim of his battered hat. He spoke in a low, croaking voice. Evan could barely hear him say in the dry air, "God help me, I did what had to be done." From that distance Evan could not see Morgan's eyes, but he could tell from his voice that they were filled with tears as well.

The old cowboy haltingly descended the steep slope toward him. Evan pressed his back to the hard rock face and couldn't bring himself to look back to where the ram lay dead in the middle of the bowl.

As Morgan got closer, Evan started to cry openly. He couldn't stop himself. "Morgan," he said, "I couldn't shoot him. I couldn't . . ."

Morgan was breathing heavily as he slid down the last few feet of the slope and halted on the ledge behind the boulder, just above Evan.

"I know," he said simply, looking down at the boy. "I was waiting for you."

"I'm sorry," Evan said, his voice shaking. "Morgan, I'm so sorry." He wasn't sure what he was sorry about, but he felt that he'd failed somehow.

Morgan clicked his teeth. "Nothin' to be sorry about. Every man has a part to play."

"What are you going to do with . . . him?" Evan asked. "You need help to get him out?"

Morgan's eyes lifted and he nodded almost imperceptivity toward the bowl.

Evan turned to follow Morgan's gaze. He consciously avoided looking at the body of the ram. There was movement on the other side of the bowl, and Evan watched as the figure of a man emerged at the edge of the grass.

"Morgan," he exclaimed as recognition set in. "That's Stone Eagle!"

Morgan pushed his hat back slightly and wiped the sweat off his forehead. "We was trackin' him too, but wanted to see what you'd do first."

Evan watched as Stone Eagle knelt by the ram and put his hand gently on the great animal's neck. His lips looked like they were chanting. He rose, grasping all four of ram's legs in his arms. Then he slowly backed off the grassy part of the plateau toward the dark black crack at the back of the bowl, pulling the ram behind him almost ceremoniously.

Evan and Morgan silently watched. Evan wanted to ask questions—he had a dozen questions—but somehow, for once, he knew that this was a time for silence. As Stone Eagle neared the crack, he turned the ram's body around and pushed it toward the darkness until it was right on the edge. He stood by the edge of the crack and removed a small leather pouch from a strap around his neck. He extended his arm in front of him and dropped the pouch onto the green grass. Then Stone Eagle carefully moved around the body and climbed down into the crack.

Evan could see only Stone Eagle's upper torso as he reached up and carefully pulled the ram with him into the crack. As the body slid out of sight Morgan said quietly, "Ain't nobody gonna make a trophy outta that ram. His time is finally over. He'll rest in peace in the Bad-lands where he belongs."

He turned to Evan. "An' nobody needs to know that he's gone. Eventually, all these outsiders will get tired and leave."

Evan nodded slightly. It didn't make complete sense to him, but it felt right in his gut. He felt a sense of calm.

Out of the corner of his eye he caught movement on the other ridge. He looked across the valley and saw the silhouette of an Indian man in traditional garb. Morgan followed Evan's eyes and gazed up at the man, too.

The Indian man raised an arm aloft. Evan looked over at Morgan and thought he saw a glint of recognition in the wrinkles around his eyes, and, perhaps, a veiled message. Morgan slowly raised his arm in response and in an instant the Indian man was gone.

Evan turned to Morgan and opened his mouth to ask a question, when an explosion, a shot from a powerful gun, filled the air, echoing around the ravine.

Evan saw shock contort Morgan's face, and knew it was how he himself looked at that moment. For the only time since he had known him, Morgan looked panicked as he reached around and fumbled with his bag.

"Morgan! Where's your .45?" Evan asked in a voice he could barely control.

Morgan held out the empty blanket in which he always wrapped the old pistol.

His eyes wide with something like terror, Morgan reached out and clapped his hand on Evan's shoulder. "Let's get up there and see if there's anything that can be done."

It took them ten minutes of hard scrambling to reach the bowl. The grass was matted down where the ram had fallen, but there were only a few spots of blood. Morgan looked at the crack and then back to Evan. He took a deep breath. "I reckon I better check to make sure what we think happened, happened."

Morgan knelt down at edge of the crack. He turned and slid his feet into the dark hole that was about three feet wide at that point.

His body slowly disappeared into the darkness until the crown of the old cowboy hat was all that could be seen. It didn't move for what seemed like a long time. Finally, the old rancher re-emerged from the darkness.

Waiting for Morgan to reappear, Evan had slipped into a kind of trance, as if this were only a very bad dream. As Morgan's gloved hands reached up, Evan snapped out of it and leaned down to help pull the old rancher out.

He helped Morgan to the flat spot on the bowl where Evan had last seen Stone Eagle and the ram. The old rancher lay on his back looking at the sky and breathing heavily. Evan sat next to him with his back to the crack waiting for him to get his breath back. Instinctively, Evan moved toward the crack to peer into the darkness. Morgan reached out and grabbed his arm. "It's enough that one of us looked," he said. "Ain't nothin but death down there."

"You gonna get your .45?" Evan asked. The second it came out of his mouth, he knew what a stupid question it was.

"I think it's done about all it can do in this world." Morgan said solemnly. "Let's get these tracks covered up and get down the ravine before our English friends come a-callin'."

Morgan sighed, rose to his feet and kicked some dust over the blood spots and pushed up the grass so the spot was camouflaged. Evan found he could do nothing but watch as Morgan brushed out the scrape marks Stone Eagle had made dragging the ram to the crack.

Evan leaned over and picked up the leather pouch Stone Eagle had dropped. Without comment he handed it to Morgan, who turned it over in his hand once before dropping it into his pocket, next to his gold watch.

Chapter Seventeen

THEY SPENT ANOTHER TEN MINUTES making certain there was no sign of humans in the bowl and started to work their way down the ravine. They worked in haste, aware that the two gunshots would have attracted the attention of anyone within a great distance. Evan led the way, pushing the pace, but stopping frequently to check on Morgan. Once they'd finished cleaning up, the old rancher seemed to drift off in a daze. He was exceptionally quiet, even for Morgan, and Evan avoided asking questions. When they got to a particularly steep bank to climb down, Morgan silently accepted Evan's outstretched arm. He seemed to have aged ten years in the last few minutes.

In forty-five minutes they were down to where the ravine ran into the main wash. Morgan turned and looked back at the two spires at the head of the ravine. He slowly tipped his hat and nodded.

"Why, Morgan? Why'd he do it?" Evan asked, his eyes filling with tears. "It don't seem right."

"Some things just come to an end, boy," he said in a dry, raspy voice. "An' some questions just aren't answered. Don't know if it's up to us to judge what's right and what's wrong. I guess he did what he felt he had to do. We'll all be judged for our actions eventually."

They heard the distant sound of riders coming down the main creek bed. Morgan snapped to life and grabbed Evan by the arm. "Let's get away from this ravine a bit." They moved up the main bed kicking their feet as they went, hoping to mess up their tracks.

"Helloooo . . ." a voice called out to them in the distance. They turned and watched a group of four riders moving up the main creek bed. Evan made out Colton, David, Lauper and Windsor. The horses were breathing hard, as if they'd been pushed.

As the group passed the place where the ravine joined the main creek bed, Evan saw David's head turn. He slowly swung his horse in that direction, further covering the tracks that led from the ravine. By the time the group caught up to Evan and Morgan, all sign of their tracks had been wiped out.

Colton reined up his tall, golden horse. "We heard a couple a shots. Did you see the sheep?" he demanded more than asked.

"Naw," Morgan drawled more slowly than usual. "The boy here flushed a deer, but I missed him."

"Damnation!" Colton exclaimed, slapping his thigh. He looked over at Evan and said, "I thought you were gonna to look for the sheep on the lowlands."

"Ummm . . . I," Evan stammered. "I was but . . . Didn't . . ."

Colton looked back at Lauper and then said to Evan. "You sure you don't want to join up with us on our hunt? You couldn't never hit the sheep with that old rifle anyway. Maybe you could help our Indian Kid find some sign."

David was about to retort, but Evan piped up, "You know, Mr. Colton, I'm getting real tired of chasin' that ol' sheep. I think he mighta' just moved on. Maybe he went to the Black Hills."

Colonel Lauper spoke in his soft English-accented voice. "It appears, Mr. Colton, that we've reached the end of another unsuccessful hunting day." He nodded at Morgan and Evan and turned his horse around.

The other riders turned their horses as well. David slid down from his mount and pulled off his bag. "Mr. Colton, you can take this horse back for me. It doesn't appear that you'll be needing my services any longer."

"If'n you leave the party here you don't get no pay for today," Colton growled. He took the reins and hurried off before David could demand any payment.

David chuckled under his breath as they watched the big figure of Colton leading the horse down the bed. "He'll put as much distance between us as possible to get out of paying me a day's wages."

Evan smiled slightly, but Morgan continued to look somber. Clearly, his mind was elsewhere. The three of them stood silently and the stillness of the Badlands enveloped them.

It was David who broke the silence, letting out a loud sigh. "So, it's over, then?" he asked in a weary voice.

Evan's eyes lit up with eagerness to tell the story, but he caught himself. He took a deep breath and just nodded.

Morgan reached into his pocket and pulled out the leather bag. "I think your pa, your real pa, wanted you to have this," he said as he held out the leather pouch to David.

He held out his hand and Morgan dropped the pouch into it. David held it in one hand for a moment, as if weighing it, then he emptied its contents into his other hand. A small carved toy horse fell out, broken into two pieces. The wood had been polished smooth. His eyes filled with tears as he held the broken toy in front of him. "How did you get it?" he asked. "Where is he?"

Evan looked at Morgan and the old cowboy studied the ground. "He's gone," he said simply.

David met Morgan's eyes. "I couldn't help him, Morgan," he said as his dark eyes clouded with tears. "I couldn't be . . . I can't be like . . . I just couldn't." He looked down at the dry sand of the streambed and tears fell at his feet.

Evan put an arm on his friend's shoulder. "No excuses, David. You do what you have to do, what you can do and then you go on," he said looking up at Morgan. The old rancher nodded and rested a hand on David's other shoulder.

The three of them kicked at the sand in the creek bed. It was uncomfortable to stay there, but none of them wanted to leave.

"So," David said, drying his eyes on the corner of his ruined white shirt. "What's next?"

They looked at each other. Finally Evan said, "Do you want to come out to Morgan's ranch? We can go back to town tomorrow. I want to tell you about the plans we made." He stopped. "I mean, if it's all right with you, Morgan?"

The old rancher smiled. "That's what partners are for, boy."

"Me an' Morgan and my pa are going to buy some of the buffalo that reporter Terrel feller told us that they have up on the Missouri Breaks," Evan said excitedly. "We're gonna raise them out on Morgan's ranch, partners like." He beamed as he looked over at Morgan.

153

"Come on," he said, putting a hand on David's shoulder. "I'll show you how we're gonna keep them and all."

David smiled and shook his head. "You'll have to show me another time, Evan."

"Are you going back East to school then?" Evan asked, trying not to show the disappointment on his face.

David looked from Evan to Morgan. "Yes, I'm going back," he said. "But not just yet."

He nodded up at the high ridge line in the spires to the west. There, silhouetted against the sky, was the figure of a man. "The voice in my dream was right. I'm going to try to find them. I have some things to learn about my past before I learn about my future."

Morgan looked up at the Indian man on the ridge, who raised his arm. The Indian man raised his arm in reply. Morgan lightly clapped David on the back and whispered, "You'll be just fine."

Evan put his hand out to shake, but David pushed it aside and embraced him with his arms. "When you get to town," he said, "tell the Blakes not to worry. I'll be back in a few weeks." Evan nodded, blinking back tears.

David turned to Morgan and firmly gripped his hand. "Thanks," was all he could whisper. The old rancher nodded his head silently.

Hoisting his bag onto his shoulder, David turned and walked down the streambed. Morgan and Evan started the other way. After a hundred yards or so, David turned and watched. Evan was talking fast and was using his arms to show Morgan something—probably about fences at their buffalo ranch, David figured. As the old rancher walked beside him, listening, David thought he could see a glint of a smile beneath his battered hat.

He turned and made his way into the heart of the Badlands.